Readers Love ANDREW GREY

Fire and Sand

"If you're looking for a lovely way to kill a cold, winter afternoon, this story will warm you up."

—Love Bytes Reviews

Fire and Glass

"One of my favorite Andrew Grey books and I have read almost all of them."

—Paranormal Romance Guild

Noble Intentions

"…very entertaining in the aspect of learning the history behind the estate and all the hidden treasures that they find."

—Gay Book Reviews

Taming the Beast

"I am enthusiastically recommending you read Taming the Beast. It has everything a perfect story needs…"

—Joyfully Jay Reviews

Redeeming the Stepbrother

"I really adore both books in this series so far, I love the fairy-tale element."

—MM Good Book Reviews

By ANDREW GREY

Published by DREAMSPINNER PRESS
www.dreamspinnerpress.com

By ANDREW GREY (cont'd)

Published by DREAMSPINNER PRESS
www.dreamspinnerpress.com

By ANDREW GREY (cont'd)

Published by DREAMSPINNER PRESS
www.dreamspinnerpress.com

FIRE AND ERMINE
ANDREW GREY

DREAMSPINNER
PRESS

Published by
DREAMSPINNER PRESS

5032 Capital Circle SW, Suite 2, PMB# 279,
Tallahassee, FL 32305-7886 USA
www.dreamspinnerpress.com

This is a work of fiction. Names, characters, places, and incidents either
are the product of author imagination or are used fictitiously, and any
resemblance to actual persons, living or dead, business establishments,
events, or locales is entirely coincidental.

Fire and Ermine
© 2023 Andrew Grey

Cover Art
© 2023 Cover Art by L.C. Chase
http://www.lcchase.com
Cover content is for illustrative purposes only and any person depicted
on the cover is a model.

Mass Market Paperback ISBN: 978-1-64108-534-2
Trade Paperback ISBN: 978-1-64108-533-5
Digital ISBN: 978-1-64108-532-8
Mass Market Paperback published March 2024
v 1.0

Printed in the United States of America
∞
This paper meets the requirements of
ANSI/NISO Z39.48-1992 (Permanence of Paper).

To Dominic, who inspires my work with the love he brings to my life.

CHAPTER 1

FRANZ REYNARD San Luis—he preferred to go by Reynard, but no one in his family abided by that—shuffled into the opulent hotel suite full of antique furniture, crystal sconces and light fixtures, and thick carpets that almost engulfed his feet. The sound from the hall outside cut off as soon as the door closed.

He released the breath he'd been holding. The dog-and-pony show he had been sent here to put on was done. He hoped they were happy. His hand ached from shaking, and his throat had grown sandy enough that it hurt to talk. Louis, one of the men traveling with him, approached, but Reynard waved him away without a word because saying anything was going to be painful.

He slumped down onto a posh sofa that had been chosen for its looks, certainly not anyone's comfort, and groaned. That was an encapsulation of his entire life: stand, look pretty, nod, do what was expected… and say what he was told to, especially in public. The person he was on the inside was immaterial and should never be shown to anyone. It was bullshit, all of it. The life he led was complete and total crap. Reynard knew he had no right to complain, though, and that was the really crappy part. Everyone else on the planet got to complain about something, but not him, because in everyone else's view, he had it all. Everything anyone could imagine… well, at least all that they thought he had. The term "gilded cage" came to mind, and the fucked-up thing was that he was the goddamned bird.

A glass of soda with ice appeared, almost by magic, on a coaster on the coffee table, and Reynard snatched it up and took a drink, and then a second, the cold liquid soothing his parched, aching throat. What he really wanted was a rich, smoky whiskey… and he wanted plenty of it. But that was out of the question. Not that he couldn't put his hands on it. All he had to do was ask and the attendant who came with the suite would produce a glass, but that was a bad idea and a slippery slope. Once he started down that, he'd pick up speed until he reached the bottom in a crash that would somehow find its way to yet another of the damned tabloid blogs that were the bane of his existence.

Langley approached the sofa and opened his planner. The man had to be the most organized person on the planet, and right now Reynard just couldn't take one more recitation of what he was going to be doing the following day. Oh, Langley was deferential and made everything sound like it was the most important day on his calendar and like Reynard had a choice, but he didn't. None at all. And that rubbed at him day in and day out. He had to do what he was told and how he was told to do it. The words out of his mouth weren't even his own but supplied by someone else.

The public ate it up, and they thought the feelings he expressed in his speeches and remarks were his own, but they weren't. Most of the time, the real person, the Reynard that he was deep down, felt like a prisoner, and he was dying to get out.

Basically, Reynard was coming to the conclusion that he had to get out before all sense of who he was as a person shriveled up and ceased to exist.

He drank some more of the fizzy liquid as he glared and shook his head at Langley. "I don't care what we're doing tomorrow or any day after that. Not right now."

"But you need to know what's going to happen," Langley said, as though whatever was on that list was the most important thing in the world.

"It will wait. All of it will." Reynard finished the soda and set the glass back down. Then he stood. "Get everyone out of the suite, now. Including you." He glared at Langley. "Everyone. I want to be able to sleep, and I'm tired of people wandering through the rest of the suite. Just give me a night of quiet and let me be alone." He waited while the attendant left the room and Langley packed up his things. Then he turned to Louis, his bodyguard of sorts, who now stood by the door. "I need to talk to you." He waited for Langley to leave.

"What is it I can do for you, Your Highness?"

He hated that Louis used his title. Louis was a generation older than Reynard and had known him since he was a boy. When he wasn't on duty, Louis would come into the nursery with a few pieces of candy to sneak to him. Some of Reynard's oldest memories were of Louis and his kindness. In a way, Louis had been his first friend. And in some ways, Louis had been his role model growing up for how a man should behave.

Lord knows it wasn't his father, who was too busy to spend a lot of time with him. Reynard understood that his father's duties took precedence. And then there was Albert, his older brother, who always came first in his parents' affections and attention. Albert was their father's heir. He had been groomed as the future of their family and would take over their father's role as king of Veronia.

At least Albert *had* a role, one created and designated by history and tradition. Reynard was the spare, the just-in-case child. His role, it seemed, was to do whatever his father, mother, or brother deigned to pass his way. At least that was how it felt.

"I need a car desperately, and I don't want Mr. Buttoned-up, Tie Me Down to know about it. No one is to. We passed a car rental outlet a block or so from the hotel. Reserve a car. I'll give you a credit card to use." Reynard went into his bedroom and located his luggage, which had been neatly stowed away. He found the piece he wanted and opened the lining to pull out a small wallet with money and credit cards inside. Then he returned to Louis. "Use this card, and you are not to tell anyone. I will never let on that you helped me in any way." Reynard would protect Louis with his last breath if he had to, just as he knew Louis would do the same for him.

"What are you going to do? New York is a huge city, and there are plenty of places where you could get into trouble without even trying."

"Then I'll get out of the city. But I have to… break out of my life for a while."

Louis shook his head. "You know I'd do just about anything for you, but this is more than just my job. If I help you, your mother and father will…."

Reynard nodded once. He knew what Louis said was the truth. His parents would freeze Louis out completely. He shouldn't have asked.

"However, I just happen to be planning a trip to see a distant relative in Scranton, and I am going to need a car. So if I happen to have a reservation for a car, I can't stop you if you take it before I get there." Louis kept his expression serious, and Reynard sighed, the tightness in his chest and stomach easing slightly.

"Thank you," Reynard said.

"But you must promise me something. Contact me occasionally to let me know that you're okay."

"I will," Reynard promised. "Thank you."

Louis left the suite, no doubt taking up a station outside the door. Reynard went into his bedroom and closed the door. He then located the cloth laundry bag he'd gotten from one of the hotel maids and packed his clothes the way he had when he'd served in the Army. There was no way he could use any of his luggage. It had all been tagged with trackers so that it could be monitored through airports and on various conveyances. He placed his things next to the bed before cleaning up, setting an alarm, and climbing into bed.

HE DIDN'T sleep much, not that he expected to. The rental car location opened at six, and Reynard was up at five thirty. No one would expect him to be awake. He was known as a late sleeper, which Reynard hoped would act to his advantage.

He dressed in worn jeans, a polo shirt, a plain tan jacket, and sneakers. He styled his hair to look like he had just gotten out of bed rather than the buttoned-up image his family insisted on. He didn't shave and hadn't the morning before as well, so his black beard had started to come in, obscuring his looks slightly. His family had rules about how they presented themselves in public, and Reynard was breaking all of them, hopefully achieving the result he needed.

Reynard moved slowly through the suite, placing the bag by the door. Then he checked the view through the peephole and found the security man on duty. His biggest issue was how to get past him to the elevator without being seen by one of the damned men in black.

He was thinking about how to create a diversion when the guard wandered down toward the end of the hall.

Reynard slipped out of the room, heading the other way, and turned the corner before the guard could notice him. He had become adept at evading guards and security as a teenager, when he'd slipped out of the royal compound on multiple occasions. He had been caught only once. "How did you do it?" his father had demanded in the voice that usually got him what he wanted.

Reynard had simply shrugged. "If I tell you then I won't be able to do it again." The logic had seemed clear enough to his teenage mind. The vein over his father's eye had throbbed, but to this day, Reynard had never told anyone his escape route.

He called for the elevator, knowing it would ding when it reached the floor and catch the guard's attention. Then he went farther down the hall, quietly slipped into the stairwell, and headed down from the sixtieth floor.

After ten floors, he was glad he was going down. Reynard slipped out of the stairwell and joined two others waiting for the elevator. He kept his gaze downward, and when the door to the empty car opened, he stepped inside. He watched the numbers on the display on the way to the lobby with the group. This particular elevator car had a round glass side, which eased Reynard's anxiety about the damned things. He hated elevators. Closed spaces didn't bother him; it was ones that moved that sent his anxiety through the roof. At least he could see out in this one. His heart raced, but finally they reached the bottom, and he smiled as he strode across the lobby and outside, where he was able to breathe in deeply.

It had rained overnight, and there was a breeze off the water that seemed to clean the city. He filled his

lungs with nonconditioned air and sighed before turning toward the car rental location, walking briskly, enjoying his first moments of freedom.

Reynard checked his Breitling watch as he moved,
knowing he had limited time to truly get away. The
clerks were just opening as he entered the rental car
location. He claimed Louis's reservation and handed
over an international driver's license with the name
that matched the one on his credit card. That had taken
some machinations and expense to get, but it was worth
it in the end.

He purchased the insurance so he was covered, and
after signing everything, he got the keys to a dark blue
BMW. Reynard stowed his bag and pulled out of the
parking structure and into Sixth Avenue traffic, following the signs to the Lincoln Tunnel. After twenty har-
rowing, nearly out-of-control traffic minutes, he was in
New Jersey, out of the city, and getting farther away by
the second.

He got onto the freeway and decided to head to
Pennsylvania and then farther west, ending up on I-78.
From there, he saw a shopping mall, where he got some
food and purchased a phone with plenty of prepaid
minutes. As far as he knew, he had a credit card that
was clean and no electronics that could be traced to him
or the palace. He'd left the damned tracked luggage behind. In short, he felt truly free for the first time in his
life. The road stretched out in front of him. All he had
to do was follow it. What could be better?

THE SUN climbed higher in the sky as Reynard flew
down the highway, satellite radio playing Handel's *Water Music*, which only added to his joy. Mile after mile

passed behind him. He had no specific destination in mind. He thought about Pittsburgh, but he bypassed the turnpike because of the tolling and cameras. Instead, he took I-78 toward I-81, figuring he could head down into Maryland and eventually Virginia. He had plenty of options, and he could choose as he wanted.

At about Allentown, he figured Langley and Louis were discovering that he was gone. The first thing Langley would do was call him. Reynard smiled at the thought of him following the ring to the bathroom, where he'd left his phone. They would have no way of tracing him. Louis would be almost as much in the dark as Langley, which would give him deniability, and that was all Reynard needed. Though he wouldn't want to be the security men assigned outside the room. Reynard was going to have to go to bat for them... eventually.

Around ten, he approached Harrisburg. He got gas off the freeway and continued on, passing south and west with the cruise control set. He was happy and content, his breathing growing easier the farther away from New York that he got. Reynard contemplated picking up I-70 when I-81 intersected it and going west. He could keep going to Denver and maybe up into Wyoming to Yellowstone. He'd always wanted to see the American West, maybe find a cowboy. With that thought, he switched stations to country music and began to sing along. He didn't know any of the words, but he sang anyway just because he felt like it.

Cowboys were sexy, and Reynard needed a little of that in his life. Well, maybe a little sex... okay, hot sex, and as much of it as he could get. The idea sent heat running through him. No one knew who he was out here. He was just another guy. He could see who he wanted and not worry if the guy sharing his bed was going to sell the story to someone the following week. *Damned Bernard.* That had been the reason he had been sent on that stupid dog-and-pony show in the first place. Get him out of Veronia for a while so the heat of the bombshell that Reynard was gay could settle down. That thought was more effective at dousing his libido than a bucket of cold water.

Lights came on behind him, blue and white, flashing in his rearview mirror. At first he didn't give them any thought. He was used to police escorts, and in Veronia, no one pulled him over. He could drive as fast as he wanted.

Except the lights *were* for him, and he wasn't in Veronia. "Shit," he muttered to himself as he slowed and pulled to the side of the road. "Great... just great."

As he pulled over, he realized he had been going too fast.

Once he came to a stop, lights lit up on the dashboard, and the engine sputtered before going silent. He tried starting it again, but the engine whirred and then the lights went dark. Great—not only was he going to have to face an American police officer, but the rental car was dead and he was stuck.

CHAPTER 2

"I HAVE A real speed demon," Fisher Bronson told Wyatt through his patrol car's speaker system. He was a rookie and had been hired on at the department less than a year ago. Wyatt had been assigned as his mentor.

"Did he stop?" Wyatt asked.

"After a few minutes, yeah. I thought at first he might run. But now it looks like the car is dead," Fisher added.

"I'm on my way, just as backup. I'll be there in less than two minutes. You know the drill, and you have this."

Wyatt was a good guy and a great trooper. Fisher considered himself lucky. He got out of the car and slowly walked up to the expensive car, which seemed to have gone completely dark. He was a little antsy, but he kept his cool.

"Do you know how fast you were going? I clocked you at seventy-five in a fifty-five zone." Fisher peered through the open window into the immaculately clean car. "I need your license, registration, and proof of insurance."

"It's a rental." The man shoved the paperwork in Fisher's direction without looking at him. That alone set Fisher on edge. Next, he pulled out a card and handed that over. Fisher looked at what the card indicated was an international license, checked out the photo, and then waited for the man in the car to turn toward him. He didn't.

That sent Fisher's suspicious nature into overdrive. He backed away and returned to the safety of his vehicle to run the plate on the car, which pulled up the information from the rental and matched the paperwork. At least part of that story was true.

Wyatt's car pulled up behind Fisher's, and he got out and came up to the window. "What do you have?"

Fisher showed him the license. "Never saw one of these before. We talked about them at the academy, though." This sort of document was rare.

"Ask him for other identification. It's likely he's a foreign national here on vacation, so request to see his passport. He can't have entered the country without one," Wyatt told him, and Fisher returned to the BMW.

"I need to see your passport, please," Fisher said, holding on to the license.

The man in the car, who the license identified as Reynard San Luis, turned to him. Fisher swallowed hard, because now that he could see him, the guy was something else, with huge brown eyes, a touch of bronze to his skin, and jet-black hair that went in every direction at once, and yet Fisher knew it had been styled that way on purpose. But what really captured his attention was the jet-black stubble on a chiseled jawline that could have been carved from stone.

He opened a small bag on the seat next to him, and Fisher tensed. Reynard pulled out a deep red folder and passed it over. Fisher took it and returned to his car.

"Jesus," he muttered as he read the name on the document. "Reynard Phillipe Henri San Luis." It was correct, if a little misleading. Reynard's actual first name, Franz, had been conveniently left off. Fisher checked the license, as well as the rental documents, before running the identification through the computer.

"Wyatt," Fisher called through the phone, "you got to see this." His hand shook as Wyatt returned from his own vehicle.

"What's so funny? Is the guy on the run? Did we locate a master criminal on one of the international watch lists?" He was being funny, but Fisher shook his head.

"No. His record doesn't come up as anything. The feds show him entering the country a week ago under a diplomatic visa."

"Okay. Give the guy a warning and tell him he needs to slow down. If he's a diplomat, he's probably got some kind of immunity, and we don't need to be the source of a diplomatic incident. Since he checks out otherwise and there isn't anything that says to apprehend him, let's just let him go."

"Okay." Fisher got his warning pad and wrote it up. "Thanks," he added, and Wyatt returned to his car and climbed inside. Fisher returned to Reynard's car, reviewed the warning, and returned his documents. "You really need to slow down. This isn't the autobahn."

"I understand. Thank you." Reynard relaxed a little and put away the documents. "Is there anyone who can help me? The car doesn't seem to want to start again."

Wyatt signaled that he was pulling out, and Fisher waved as he drove off. Then he returned to the handsome driver. "Is there a number on the paperwork for the rental car company? They should send someone out to help you." Fisher looked over the documents and waited while Reynard made the call. "Do you want to pop the hood? I can look for you."

Reynard nodded, and Fisher lifted the hood and spotted the issue right away. One of the cables had come unhooked from the battery. Fisher put on a work glove from his car's emergency kit and carefully reattached the cable. He was able to get it to stay, but he wasn't sure how long it would remain there. The battery coupling was broken and needed to be repaired. He lowered the hood and relayed that to Reynard.

"Is there somewhere I can take the car so the rental company can bring out a replacement vehicle?" Reynard asked. His voice was soft and gentle, like one of those confident people who was used to being listened to and never needed to raise his voice.

"Go up to the next exit and take a right. You'll see a shopping center with a large parking lot. You'll be out of traffic and should be able to get some food and stuff while you wait."

Reynard sighed. "Is there a hotel or something? I might as well stay for a day or two until this gets straightened out."

"There's the Comfort Suites downtown. It's pretty nice, and they have a parking garage with a valet." Reynard nodded. "I can lead you there if you want to follow me."

"Thank you," Reynard said, finally smiling like he meant it.

Fisher returned to his patrol car, waited for traffic to clear, and then eased out and took the lead down the half mile to the exit before heading through town. Fisher hoped the car made it until they reached the hotel.

In front of the new building in the historic town he called home, Fisher pulled into a parking space and motioned for Reynard to turn in, waiting for him to get off the street and roll down his window. "Are you okay?"

"They have a room, and I should be fine. Thank you for your assistance," he said before making the left turn into the drive.

Fisher was still on duty, so he continued through town, returned to the freeway, and took up his position in the median, where he could be seen and clock the speed of passing vehicles for the next three hours until his shift ended. Lord help police officers who went into this line of work for the excitement.

"YOU DID really well today," Wyatt said after Fisher had changed out of his uniform and was getting set to head home from the station. Most state police troopers didn't work out of a station. They handled their territory from their car. But since Fisher's territory included Carlisle, and because it overlapped with Wyatt's, at least for now, there was a station for him to work out of. Fisher had no illusions—once this initial settle-in period was over, his territory would change and he would spend his days working out of his cruiser. He had been told that his assignment would be in the area, which was a relief to himself, as well as his grandmother.

For over half the area of the state of Pennsylvania, especially in rural areas and some tiny communities, the state police were the only law-enforcement presence. That made the job he and his fellow troopers were doing even more critical.

"Thanks," Fisher said as they left the station.

"You kept your cool and weren't afraid to ask questions." He and Wyatt had already gone over all of the stops he had made that day to review procedures. Fisher felt pretty good about what he'd done, and he stood tall as he headed for his truck to go home.

The drive across town took ten minutes, and then he pulled into the driveway of his grandmother's home on Bedford Street. He loved the bungalow-style house that she and his grandfather had bought shortly after they married many decades ago and had cared for ever since. His grandfather loved cars, so over the years, the single-stall garage had been built onto, and now there were three bays. Fisher parked his F-150 in the middle one. His grandmother's Escape sat in the first bay, and the last one had his grandfather's '67 Mustang under a car cover to keep the dust off.

"You're home in one piece," his grandmother said as she appeared in the doorway that led to her impressive backyard. She was a member of the garden club and spent a lot of her time in the yard. Fisher did the heavy work for her, but she got him out of the way when it came to her plants.

"Yes, I'm home," he told her, giving his gran a hug. She and Gramps had raised him after his mother passed away when he was sixteen. His father had never been in the picture. Gramps passed last year, so now it was just him and Gran. Fisher had thought about moving out, but his grandmother needed help, and he had the entire upper floor, with its large bedroom and a second area that he could use as a workspace to himself. "How was your day? It looks like you got the new bed planted."

"I did, and I'm happy with it." She smiled, but her eyes had lost some of that spark. It was probably to be expected after having Gramps for fifty-three years. She took off her gloves and set them in her gardening cart. "I made some macaroni salad, and I'm going to cook burgers for dinner. Go on in and get yourself cleaned up, and—"

Sirens sounded out on Hanover, first one unit and then more, building to a cacophony. Fisher checked his phone and dialed in to dispatch. "What's happening downtown?" he asked the operator.

"A big fire at the hotel downtown. Apparently they have evacuated the building and have called in a number of units."

"Do they need help?" Fisher asked.

"We haven't been called, but assistance couldn't hurt. They are going to need people to route traffic, and it takes time to get everyone in."

"I've got to go, Gran," Fisher told her before racing inside. He got a clean uniform pulled on before kitting up. Then he headed out and drove the eight blocks to where a phalanx of fire trucks and emergency vehicles filled the street. Smoke billowed skyward as he sped up and approached the officer in charge. "How can I help? Trooper Fisher Bronson."

"Can you help get the guests moved away from the hotel and down the street?"

"Can do. I'll contact the Red Cross, see if they can assist with anything." These were folks away from home and now out of their hotel with just the clothes they were wearing, and judging by the smoke, no one was going to be returning to the hotel anytime soon.

Fisher made the call and was informed that they were already gearing up. He then joined the milling guests. "Please move on back a little farther," he told the crowd and got them moving down the sidewalk away from the scene.

"When can we go back to the hotel?" one man asked.

"I don't know," Fisher answered, guiding them back as more clouds of smoke and steam rose into the sky. Firefighters were pumping a ton of water onto the blaze.

"There's a hotel out on Carlisle Pike near the turnpike that has rooms," another man said. "I got one reserved, and I have them on the phone." He passed it to another man, who spoke with the staff and passed the phone back. He shared his device until the hotel filled up. Those lucky enough to get rooms made their way out of downtown to get an Uber, which left a smaller group—one more confused and worried.

"I know you," Fisher said, taking a second to recognize the guy he'd pulled over.

"Yeah. You didn't give me a citation today," he said, watching the hotel. "My rental car company is going to be thrilled about this."

"Did they replace your car?" Fisher asked.

"Yes. An hour ago. Now it's stuck in the garage behind the building." He shrugged.

"The hotels out by the hospital are full," another of the waiting guests said, and the last few people sighed. "So are the B and Bs in town."

Reynard's shoulders slumped and he slipped his phone back into his pocket. "Maybe once I have the car…."

The workers from the Red Cross arrived and set up a table with coffee and sandwiches. At least folks and the firefighters were getting fed.

The smoke rising into the air dwindled, and firefighters exited the building. It seemed to Fisher that they most likely had the fire out and were checking out the inside of the building, but that wouldn't do any of these people any good. They might be able to get their things, but no one was going to be sleeping in that building tonight or in the foreseeable future. The displaced guests continued making calls, with some of them able to locate beds for the night.

"What are you going to do?" Fisher asked Reynard when it became clear that he was one of the few left standing. The floundering look he received in response told Fisher all he needed to know.

CHAPTER 3

ALL REYNARD'S plans were going up in smoke right in front of him. The damned fire alarm had gone off just as he got settled into his room. He'd run out to find smoke in the hallways, and now he was out on the street.

"Thank you," a woman said as a man shook Reynard's hand.

"You're welcome," Reynard said automatically. Manners had been drilled into him since he was able to speak, and the words just came out. "Though I'm not sure what I did," he added gently.

"You got us out of the building," the man said. "We couldn't see anything, and my wife was choking. You took her by the hand and led the both of us out of that death trap." He smiled brightly as one of those huge American gas guzzlers pulled up to the corner.

"You're okay," a young woman said. She jumped out and hugged both of them as tears began on all sides. "I told you both you should have stayed with us." She was already herding what Reynard assumed were her parents into the vehicle. "Let's get you home and you can clean up and rest. We'll get the luggage later."

Reynard stepped back as they climbed into the vehicle. They waved, and then the doors closed and the driver backed up toward the cordoned-off area before turning around and heading back down the otherwise empty street.

"It seems you were a hero," Trooper Bronson said. Reynard got the name from the tag on his uniform.

Reynard smiled. "Not really. I knew we needed to get out, so I guess I took their hands and dragged them along with me to the stairs I'd used earlier." His hatred of elevators had come in handy, because he knew exactly where the stairs were located. "It wasn't anything that anyone else wouldn't have done."

A fireman in uniform approached and spoke to Trooper Bronson. Reynard wished he knew the man's first name. The trooper was handsome, and he had these large puppy-dog eyes that drew Reynard in. He also liked the way the trooper filled out that uniform. He had known for a while that he had a kink for that kind of thing—a man in a formfitting, neatly pressed uniform just did it for him. There was something about the hint of the man underneath, the way a man's muscles filled the pant leg or the hint of bicep when he moved. His first awakening of attraction had been to a ceremonial guard at the family's country retreat who filled out the red-and-black uniform in the most spectacular way.

Reynard smiled to himself as he remembered playing in the forest at the edge of the estate and coming across that particular guard bathing in one of the hidden mountain lakes. Not only had a young Reynard finally realized what he had been trying to deny about himself, but he also learned that his imagination sometimes paled in comparison to reality.

"Do you have a place to stay?" Trooper Bronson asked, pulling Reynard out of his memories.

"No," he answered, slipping his hand into his pocket and sliding his fingers over his phone. All he needed to do was make a call to Louis and someone would be here in a matter of hours to pick him up and return him to New York and the very cage he had been trying to escape. God, this little jaunt had indeed taught him how ill-prepared he truly was for the real world. Here he was standing on a street corner after a damned hotel fire. Everyone around him had gotten on their phones to arrange a place to stay, and he had done nothing. Reynard had simply expected that someone would tell him where he was supposed to go. That was his life. He didn't do things for himself on a daily basis. He had Langley to keep his schedule and make any arrangements he needed. If he wanted to go somewhere, there was always a driver to take him. When he wanted to drive, the garage kept his cars ready and in tip-top shape. "I guess I should see if I can get my car."

"The garage is still blocked off and probably will be for a while. It's a mess with debris from the fire, and it got flooded with water from the overspray. It's going to take time to clean up, and it isn't a priority right now," a nearby firefighter said. He exchanged a look with Trooper Bronson and then returned to where the rest of his team was working to gather up their equipment.

Firefighters came and went from the building. Reynard watched, wondering if he should give up and just make the call. He could probably get Langley to say that Reynard had spent the day sightseeing in the city and that he was back. His family didn't need to know what he'd done, and he could return to the daily suffocation that was his life.

"What room were you in?" the trooper asked.

"Three-one-two," Reynard answered.

The trooper nodded and strode over to where the firefighters were congregating as some of them got ready to leave. One of them broke away from the group and went into the hotel. A few minutes later he came out with Reynard's white laundry bag. The trooper said something and then returned to hand the bag to Reynard.

"Is this all you had?" he asked.

Reynard nodded and opened it, relieved that the clothes didn't smell like smoke, though the outside of the bag did. "Thank you." At least he had some clothes and a few of his things. Reynard still couldn't get to his car, and he had no place to stay, but this was progress.

The emergency services were packing up, and even the Red Cross had finished and were heading away. Reynard stood on the sidewalk, his bag near his feet, trying to figure out his next move.

"Look, the hotels are all full, and it's getting late. The fire department is going to need to assess the cause of the fire and then check out the entire building before they can possibly let anyone inside, and that could take days."

Reynard shrugged. "I have my stuff. All I need is the car." Then he could figure out if he should head back to New York or continue on his journey, though his first day away was not a good indicator by any means. His car breaking down and the hotel catching fire were probably signs that he should go back with his tail between his legs.

"Well, it's getting dark, and nothing more will happen tonight. My grandmother and I have an extra room, so you can stay with us for tonight."

Reynard was so relieved. "Are you sure I'm not going to be a bother?"

"It's one night, and you seem like a nice enough guy. Besides, I'm a police officer." The last words were uttered more deeply and with a hint of the banked strength that probably went with his uniform. "My truck is over here." He motioned, and Reynard headed down to the vehicle. The trooper followed him after speaking to the officer in charge.

"I'm Fisher, by the way."

"Reynard," he answered. It would have been rude to simply assume that the trooper remembered his name from earlier. And the truth was, he didn't want to be that memorable. He was trying to escape his life for a while, not leave a trail a mile wide.

Fisher extended his hand, and Reynard hesitated for a second before taking it. In his world, he initiated all physical contact, and handshakes were done in public situations where he had control. It wasn't a casual greeting. But this was America, and he could try to fit in.

"Come on, get in the truck," Fisher said with a smile.

"Do you work outside the police force?" Reynard asked as he climbed into the vehicle.

"No," Fisher answered, sounding a little confused.

"Then what do you use the truck for?" He turned around, expecting the bed to be filled with wood or stone or other stuff that needed hauling, but it was as clean and shiny as the rest of it. "Back home, these aren't as big and would be used for work." People didn't just drive trucks for fun.

"I use it to help Gran and stuff. Mostly I drive it because I like being a little higher than in a car." He pulled out and used back streets, passing a school and a cemetery and eventually turning into a neighborhood and then pulling into a garage. The door slid down behind them. "Come on inside. Gran is going to be thrilled to meet you."

"Why?" Reynard asked, wondering if Fisher had figured out who he was.

"Gran doesn't get out as much as she used to."

He led them out of the garage and into a yard filled with color. Roses and flowers of every description filled the beds that lined the yard. It was a riot of color to rival any of the gardens at home.

"Who's this?" an elderly woman asked from the back door.

"Reynard San Luis. He was staying at the hotel downtown and got burned out. There's nothing else available, so I've invited him to spend the night here, and we'll figure things out tomorrow."

"I see," she said a little coldly, as though she wasn't sure about him or having a stranger in her home.

"Your garden is magnificent," Reynard said, turning on the charm. "One of the prettiest I've seen in a long time." He set down his bag and wandered to a patch of soft pink iris next to deep purple ones. "Your use of color is amazing."

"Do you garden?" she asked, her lips curling upward. "I've done it all my life. I used to grow vegetables when this one was a boy, but I converted all that to flowers years ago."

"Not like this," he answered. The truth was that he used to watch the gardeners on the estate, but of course he never worked with them. "Maybe you could show me some of your favorites if you have time." Darkness was falling quickly, and soon very little was going to be visible, but that didn't detract from the loveliness around him.

She nodded. "You should come inside." Her gaze went down to the bag. She looked at it for a few seconds and then opened the door. "Fisher can show you the guest room, and then you can clean up. Did you eat before the fire?"

Reynard's stomach rumbled at the thought of food. He had ordered room service, but it hadn't arrived by the time he had had to evacuate his room. "Excuse me," he said, embarrassed. "I didn't get a chance."

"I see." She turned to Fisher. "Take him where he can get settled, and I'll warm something up for both of you."

"Thanks, Gran," Fisher said, kissing her cheek, and she smiled—really smiled—for the first time since their unexpected guest had arrived. "You're the best, and you know I couldn't just leave anyone standing on the sidewalk. You taught me better than that." He hugged her gently, and Reynard saw her melt before his eyes. Fisher could most definitely give lessons in charm.

"Go on with you," she said, and Fisher led the way to a back bedroom on the first floor. It was small but comfortable. Reynard appreciated the hospitality.

"The bathroom is right outside. I'll meet you in the kitchen in a few minutes."

Reynard wondered why the kitchen. He had never spent much time in kitchens since he was a kid. If he was hungry, he simply rang for what he wanted and someone brought it to him. Maybe this was some sort of American thing. Shrugging, he cleaned up and put his bag next to the bed and followed the voices to the kitchen.

Fisher sat at the table, with his grandmother putting things in the oven. Reynard sat down across from Fisher and smiled. Manners told him to go with whatever happened and to be grateful. These people were helping him, and after all, this was what he wanted. Reynard was out of the gilded cage and had to exist on his own. That meant experiencing new things and meeting new people. There weren't going to be any of the trappings of royalty or the things that only lots of money could buy.

"I really appreciate your help. Thank you," Reynard said.

"You're welcome."

The room filled with the scent of whatever was in the oven, and his belly rumbled again. "That smells amazing."

"It's Gran's corn pudding. The stuff is to die for. She grew up in Virginia and is the best cook in the country. Maybe if we're really nice she'll make her fried green tomatoes or her chicken. They're both out of this world." Fisher licked his lips.

"This one is such a sweet talker," Gran said, patting his hand. "Would you go downstairs and get me some of the peaches I put up last year?"

Fisher got up and left the room to tromp down the stairs.

Gran sat at the table. "Okay, young man, what's your story?" She narrowed her gaze. "Are you on the run from someone? Fisher is a good trooper with a kind heart… and I know someone who's too nervous and fidgety for their own good."

"I'm not on the run—as you say—from anyone. I'm taking a road trip for a while." That was as close to the truth as he wanted to get. "You have nothing to worry about."

She shook her head. "I know you aren't in trouble with the law. Fisher would have shaken that out of you if you were. What I'm wondering is why someone as genteel and cultured as you are is here in town. And don't go giving me the BS about your car."

The police back home could use this woman to break anyone they suspected of a crime. Heck, Reynard was tempted to tell her everything, and he had just met her. This was one formidable lady.

"I wanted to travel and see some things before I have to go back home and do what's expected." The thought of returning left him cold.

"I see. Born with a silver spoon and can't figure shit out." She rolled her eyes. "You young people do too much thinking and soul-searching. Maybe if you were grateful and happy with what you got, you'd be happier." She leaned closer, and Reynard wondered if she could see into him. It was strange, but he swore she could almost see all his secrets.

Footsteps sounded on the stairs. "Are these what you were looking for?" Fisher asked. Gran nodded and took the jar, then returned to the counter, much to Reynard's relief. She went back to the oven, and after a few more minutes began setting out dishes that looked like nothing Reynard had ever had before and yet smelled like heaven.

"Can you boys clean up after yourselves? I'm going to go to bed. I had a busy day in the garden," Gran said.

"Of course," Fisher told her and Reynard did the same, waiting while Fisher kissed her cheek before she left the room. Only then did Reynard sit back down.

"Why did you stand?" Fisher asked.

"Because a lady left the room," Reynard answered. His mother would have laid into him if he hadn't. Fisher began filling his plate, and Reynard waited his turn, then took a little of each dish. "Does she always cook like this?" He tried the corn pudding and closed his eyes in delight. Corn was something that was never served at home. Any corn they grew was animal feed, but this was sweet, yet savory, smooth, and…. He had no words.

"Not always, no," Fisher answered, biting his lower lip. "She loves to cook, but she has days where she isn't able. Gran loves to garden, cook, and she'll have a clean house if it kills her, but sometimes she overdoes it." He turned to look down the hall. "I worry about her."

"I know how you feel. My father's mother was very special. She was always very fussy about how we behaved in public, but was the first to sneak into the nursery with sweets of some sort. I remember her sitting with my brother and me, telling us stories." He smiled and received a warm one from Fisher in return. "Did you always want to be a police officer?" Reynard asked, figuring a change of subject was a good idea. He didn't want Fisher asking too much about his family if he could help it.

"As far back as I can remember. I was a criminal justice major in college, and then I went to the state police academy. I did very well, top of my class, and when the opening came up here, I applied so I could stay close to Gran." He ate a few more bites, his gaze warming. Damn, he was stunning, even in civilian clothes. Full lips, a hint of skin at the collar, intelligent eyes that Fisher was pretty sure missed very little. Reynard wondered what would happen if Reynard showed an overt interest. Probably not a particularly good idea.

"What would you have done if you had had to move to another area of the state?" Reynard asked.

Fisher shrugged. "I'd probably have gone there and driven back on my days off to help Gran. She's the only family I have."

Reynard was used to people being nice to him, even to the point of sucking up. It came with his position. But Fisher and his grandmother had no idea who he was, and yet they were being nice. All his life, Reynard had been told—even had it drilled into him—to choose his friends carefully and that he should be wary of what others wanted from him. As a teenager, he had thought he knew better and become friends with one of the kids at Eton whose father was a British industrialist. Turned out, Meyer's family was trying to use the relationship between the two of them to their advantage in a negotiation with a company in Veronia. It got messy, and in the end Reynard was pulled out of the school and sent to another in Switzerland.

He didn't have to worry about that sort of thing with Fisher and his grandmother. Heck, very few people outside his family ever spoke to him the way Fisher's gran had. She was honest and intense—a refreshing attitude in a life where subterfuge and ulterior motives to curry favor and influence were constant concerns.

"What's your family like?" Fisher asked.

How did he answer? "A pain in the backside most of the time. They have all these expectations of what I'm supposed to do and how I should act. I loved science and wanted to be an architect, but my father didn't approve and sent me to study economics. Can you imagine anything more boring? I spent four years studying theories that most of the time have little to do with the real world. It was enough to make my head spin, but I did it because it was what was expected."

Fisher set his fork on the plate. "And you always do what's expected?"

Reynard leaned over the table like he was sharing a secret. "Most of the time." Damn, he loved the way

Fisher's eyes widened and his lips curled in a smile that brought out dimples in his cheeks. Reynard had never seen someone with real smile dimples before. Heat ignited from the base of his spine as a pull he couldn't explain drew him closer to Fisher.

He wanted this man—and most of the time that would be no problem. Lots of guys wanted to go to bed with a prince. Sometimes Reynard thought it was a bucket-list item. Collect a royal fuck flush. Bang a baron, check. Copulate with a count, check. Diddle a duke, check. Eat out an earl, check. Pork a prince, check… check. The only thing higher on the totem pole was to kink it up with a king, but that just brought up thoughts of his father and… ew. It would be nice, though, for someone to be interested in him for who he was. But maybe that was more than Reynard had a right to expect.

CHAPTER 4

FISHER WATCHED Reynard closely. There was something intriguing, maybe a bit dangerous, about him. It hadn't escaped his notice that Reynard seemed uncomfortable talking about himself and that he was good at changing the subject. But damn, those eyes… there was something that drew him in, but it gave him pause at the same time. It wasn't pain he saw, but maybe deep-down unhappiness. This was likely a man adrift in his own life and trying to find his path. That was something he understood. Fisher had been blessed with knowing exactly what he wanted to do, but his personal life had been hard to come to grips with. Gran was old-school in many ways, and he had dreaded telling her he was gay.

For a long time he did his best to ignore his feelings, hoping they would change or go away. Fisher had hoped that as he got older, he would be able to be like most everyone else.

"So it's just you and Gran?" Reynard said, in a half-questioning sort of way.

"Yeah. There's no one else in my life right now. Hasn't been for a while," Fisher answered. "Not since David, and that was a disaster." The words slipped out, and for a second Reynard smiled, and then his expression grew serious once again.

"I'm sorry. But I think we all have at least one asshole in our pasts. Mine was Pierre. I thought it was real between us and, well…." He trailed off and shrugged. "My grandmother would say that we can't let our past dictate our future... but it's hard sometimes."

"Gran hated David on sight. At first I thought it was because of the whole guy thing...." Fisher swallowed hard to wet his dry throat as the realization that what he had been hoping was true set in. Pierre had to be a guy, and that meant that the butterflies in his belly had been telling him that Reynard was interested in other men. "But it turned out that Gran didn't have too hard a time with that. At least not the way I expected." He leaned forward. "She can be a little set in her ways."

Reynard glanced toward the ceiling. "I wouldn't have expected that."

Fisher chuckled. His gran didn't pull punches, and she was usually right, even when Fisher wished she wasn't. "David was one of those guys who fell for the uniform, and he thought it would be exciting to date a cop. But the reality was different than he expected. I work long hours and come home tired. David wanted to go out and party the nights away, and I couldn't do that. He also wanted me to turn a blind eye to the things his friends were doing, and I couldn't do that either." He ate the last of his dinner and pushed the plate back. "When one of his friends pulled out a bag of cocaine and started passing it around, David expected me to walk away." David had had the ability to compound dumb on top of stupid and expect everything to be okay.

"What did you do?" Reynard asked, his perfect lips parted in surprise,

For a second, Fisher lost his train of thought. "I called in the police and held all of them until they arrived. It turned out one of David's friends was a midlevel distributor, and they were able to get him to flip. I was still in training at that point, but it was a real feather in my cap. David never spoke to me again, and I was better off without him. Gran practically did a happy dance in the living room. I wouldn't do anything different if I had it to do over." He knew that deep down. If he had turned a blind eye, then it would have been selling his soul for David, and Fisher could never do that.

"I'd like to think I'd do the same thing you did if I was in your position. We have stuff like that back home too, and it tears apart people's lives." Reynard's eyes blazed, and Fisher found the conviction and intensity sexy as all hell.

"I know it was the right thing, but it still hurt that David cared so little about me," Fisher said.

"There are jerks everywhere. Pierre... well, he just wanted me for what I could do for him. Nothing more," Reynard said as though it were nothing, but the hurt that flashed in his eyes told Fisher there was more to it. He also got the vibe that there were a lot of things Reynard wasn't saying. That sent his police officer curiosity running.

Fisher didn't know much about this man other than he was here on a diplomatic visa. He seemed nice enough and had exceptional manners, but other than that he was just a guy who had needed a place to stay. The fact that Fisher found him so attractive and could lose himself in Reynard's eyes only set him on edge more. He wanted to know what Reynard looked like under his expensive shirt and jeans that probably cost what he and Gran spent on food in a month.

But people were entitled to their secrets. Fisher knew that, and Reynard didn't owe him his life story. As long as he was a well-behaved guest, that was all Fisher could expect. But something was a little... not off, but *different* about Reynard. Maybe that was the attraction?

Reynard finished eating, and Fisher took care of the dishes. Then he turned out the lights and they went into the living room, where he found something on Netflix.

FISHER FOUND himself glancing at Reynard every few seconds. They were watching an old action movie, and Reynard leaned forward almost the entire time. "Is that how people really drive here?"

Fisher smiled. "I hope not. It's just a movie. But these are fun, even if the good guys make the police look stupid most of the time." He settled back as Reynard watched, jumping at the spectacular car crashes and wild antics.

After the movie drew to a close, Fisher turned off the television, and Reynard thanked Fisher again and said good night before going down the hall to the guest room. Fisher stayed up to turn out the lights before heading up the stairs to go to bed. He wondered how Reynard would react if Fisher knocked on his door. He liked to think that Reynard would invite him in and kiss him senseless as soon as the door was closed. Heat built inside him, and his hand shook a little as he opened the door to his bedroom. His imagination was in overdrive. Maybe he had been watching too much porn or something.

Porn always had the weirdest meetups, with guys looking at each other and then… boom-chicka-mow-mow. Not only was Fisher not going to show up at Reynard's door, but to Fisher that would seem like he was asking for sex as some sort of payment for the room. No way was that happening, so he went to his bathroom and cleaned up before going to his room, where he finished getting undressed and climbed into bed.

He wished he was able to sleep, but his mind kept running in circles. Fisher lay there staring at the ceiling, hoping his brain would quiet. After an hour, he considered reading or surfing the internet on his computer. He pushed back the covers and climbed out of bed, but a soft noise from downstairs drew his attention. Gran sometimes had trouble sleeping and she wandered the house, which always concerned him. Fisher pulled on a pair of loose shorts and quietly went downstairs.

The door to Gran's room was closed, but there was water running in the kitchen. Fisher went through and stopped in the doorway. Reynard stood at the sink in dark silken sleep pants and nothing else. Damn, his clothes had most definitely hidden the mouthwatering hotness well.

Reynard started and turned around, a glass of water in one hand.

"Sorry, I heard someone down here and thought Gran might be wandering." Fisher took in Reynard's chest… and the dusting of black hair across his pecs and down his belly that disappeared into the elastic band at his waist. What Fisher noticed next was the way Reynard was returning the look. He slowly raised the glass to his lips and drank the last of the water, his biceps bunching as he moved. Holy hell, this

was one stunning man, and he was watching Fisher
as though he were a meal and Reynard was starving.

Fisher knew as soon as he moved forward that
this was probably a mistake, but he'd denied himself
enough. Reynard set the glass on the counter without
shifting his gaze. Fisher's heart beat faster, and his
breathing became shallow. Without thinking, he swallowed hard and closed the distance between them. It
took mere seconds before Fisher had Reynard in his
arms, kissing him ferociously. Blessedly, Reynard gave
as good as Fisher did, meeting all of his energy and
passion.

"Damn," Reynard gasped when Fisher pulled
away to breathe.

"Fuck," Fisher moaned, and then they were on
each other again, the kiss almost bruising. Reynard
tasted like rich heat, and Fisher wanted more. Without
breaking their kiss, he guided Reynard out of the room
and toward the stairs, desperate to hold on.

At the base of the stairs, Fisher released Reynard,
took him by the hand, and quietly led him up the stairs
and to his room. He didn't want to think about what
Gran would say if she knew, but at the moment, all his
blood was racing south and he wasn't really thinking
anyway.

As soon as the bedroom door closed, Fisher pressed
Reynard toward the bed. They fell onto the mattress
together, with Reynard holding him as their kissing intensified. Man, Reynard knew how to kiss, sending the
temperature between them to white-hot.

"God," Fisher groaned as he slid his hand down
Reynard's powerful back, loving the way his muscles
quivered under his touch. There was something hot-
ter than hell about that kind of reaction, and when he

slipped his hand into Reynard's sleep pants and over his firm ass, Fisher found himself groaning again. This was a man who had to have done squats until he could barely hold himself up.

"You can say that again," Reynard whispered as he pushed at Fisher's shorts.

It didn't take long before they were both naked, and the temperature in the room rose even more. Fisher held Reynard's arms and brought them up over his head, holding his intense gaze.

"What are you doing?" Reynard asked, not fighting his hold.

"I'm going to drive you crazy." He drew closer, Reynard's hot breath ghosting over his skin. "We have to be quiet, so no matter how much you want to scream your passion to the ceiling, remember that Gran is right downstairs." He kissed him before Reynard could say anything, then pulled away.

The sexiest thing ever was the way Reynard kept his hands up over his head even once Fisher let go. What an incredible sight—that strong man laying himself out like that for Fisher. His cock throbbed.

"Holy hell," he whispered, tweaking one of Reynard's pert, tawny nipples before taking it between his lips and laving as Reynard shook under him.

"I take it you like to be in charge," Reynard said. "That's fine, but…."

"Nothing to worry about. I'm not into pain or anything. I just like to be the one to call the shots." Honesty was best, especially at a time like this when they had just met. Reynard's eyes widened, and he nodded slowly. "I'm not going to hold you down. This is all up to you." He slipped his hands down Reynard's strong chest and his fluttering belly to his ample cock.

After wrapping his fingers around the length, he stroked slowly as Reynard moaned softly. "Oh hell," Reynard moaned. "Damn, this is so good."

Fisher smiled and squeezed more firmly before stopping his strokes and taking Reynard between his lips, sucking him deep. Reynard groaned long and low, not moving other than his cock twitching, as Fisher sank deeper. Reynard tasted sweet-salty, and Fisher slowly worked Reynard's uncut cock between his lips, sucking hard as he pulled away, adding pressure as he bobbed his head.

Reynard nearly came unglued under him, and that only increased Fisher's desire for this man. He was strong yet responsive, a real hedonist, soaking up the care that Fisher gave him like a sponge. Fisher couldn't help wondering how long it had been since anyone had shown Reynard this kind of attention.

"Fisher…." Reynard groaned deeply as he touched his head. "I'm so close."

Fisher eased away, writhing as Reynard heaved for breath and fell back on the pillows, almost wrung out, eyes wide. Fisher slid up him, loving that Reynard kept his arms over his head.

When Reynard gave himself over to him, Fisher knew it was his duty—no, *joy*—to make sure Reynard received all the pleasure possible. He loved the way his eyes widened with each touch and the way his own skin tingled as his chest pressed to Reynard's, their lips finding each other's in the dark.

Reynard wrapped his legs around Fisher's waist, and Fisher let his hands roam down Reynard's thighs, caressing and exploring, teasing and loving the hard strength under his touch. This man was near physical perfection. Fisher figured that tomorrow he'd be gone and Fisher would never see him again, so he gave everything he had, opening himself more than he should have to Reynard. He did it because it wasn't going to matter. Fisher could give all he had because when Reynard was gone, he would go back to the life he had before. This was one night of unbridled passion where Fisher was free to be who he wanted and give what he wanted.

He reached to the bedside and found one of the packets he kept at the back. Using his teeth, he tore it open and then rolled the condom onto his length. Then he prepared Reynard to soft moans and even whimpers. "What are you waiting for?"

"Need to get you ready," Fisher whispered in a rush, everything driving him forward.

"I am. Just… take me." He pressed back as Fisher pushed forward, breaching him and then sinking into tight heat that threatened to overwhelm him.

Fisher growled as Reynard rose to meet him, the kiss heated as their bodies came together. He swore his head was going to float away from the intensity. This was passion, and Fisher wouldn't have been surprised if the two of them scorched the sheets. As it was, Reynard's body gripped him, drawing him deeper. And when he moved, Reynard kept time with him.

"Don't stop," Reynard whimpered, bringing his arms down and around Fisher's back. They rocked together, holding each other, the light from the street outside just enough for the desire in Reynard's eyes to shine. "Damn…."

"Are you okay?"

"Fuck yeah," Reynard hissed. "Don't you dare stop."

Fisher picked up the pace, and Reynard did the same, both of them breathing at the same intervals. It was astonishing how in sync they were with each other as he drove deep and then held still, cock jumping. He had to stop or else he was going to lose control. No one had ever done that to him before. Fisher prided himself on knowing his own mind and body, but Reynard threw all of that out the window. It seemed they both knew what they wanted and how to make it happen.

"Fisher," Reynard groaned. "Don't…." He gasped, and his voice grew more desperate.

Fisher knew Reynard was close; hell, he was seconds from instinct completely taking over. His control stretched, but Fisher wanted this to last. Still, there was only so much he could do, especially as Reynard clamped his eyes closed, body shaking under him.

Fisher leaned forward and kissed Reynard as he stilled and shook through his release. Fisher held on as long as he could, but the sight of Reynard enveloped in pleasure was too much, and he plummeted into passion that seemed to go on forever.

FISHER HELD still, breathing deeply, just holding Reynard as they huffed like racehorses in the otherwise quiet room. He didn't want to move, but their bodies had other ideas, and they both squirmed as they disconnected. Fisher got up and took care of the condom before climbing back into bed.

"We should probably talk," Reynard said. "There are things that I should…."

Fisher snuggled closer. "How about we do that in the morning?" he offered, resting his head on Reynard's shoulder. "It's late and, well… let's just… I don't know… let whatever this was be special… at least for now." Fisher had no idea what this meant, but he didn't want to pop the magic bubble around them. That would happen quickly enough. Reynard put his arms around him, and Fisher sighed and closed his eyes, sleep overtaking him quickly.

Hours later, light flooded the room, and Fisher woke to find he was alone. He sat up before figuring that Reynard had probably returned to the guest room so they wouldn't have to face Gran's questions. Not that he could blame him. Fisher got up and used the bathroom, shaving and brushing his teeth before going downstairs.

Gran was in the kitchen already, making breakfast. "Is your guest still asleep?" she asked without turning away from the stove.

"I'll check." Fisher went down the hall. The guest room door was open, with Reynard's bag on the bed. At least he hadn't left, though Fisher wouldn't have expected that of Reynard. He always had good manners, and sneaking out would be bad form, even if Fisher wasn't sure what to say to him after last night.

They had had an amazing time together, and Fisher had felt a connection with Reynard he hadn't with other guys—except maybe David, but that had been one-sided. Maybe this was the same, not that it mattered. Reynard was passing through town, and Fisher didn't need to let himself get all mushy. They'd had a great night, one Fisher would remember, but he reminded himself not to make too much out of it.

"Good morning," Reynard chirped as he came out of the bathroom, moving a little stiffly. "Thank you for letting me stay…." Reynard leaned closer. "And for last night. You were amazing." He smiled and then kissed him quickly. Fisher smiled warmly, and for a second, it was returned.

"Boys, breakfast," Gran called, and almost immediately, Reynard's expression changed. It didn't turn cold exactly, but a kind of blandness washed over him, like he was just… there.

"Coming, Gran," Fisher called, and motioned for Reynard to go first.

Once at the table, Gran dished up eggs with ham and some of her special hash browns—crunchy on the outside and soft in the middle. She set plates in front of both of them, giving Fisher a stern look as she did. Then she got a plate for herself and sat down. A coffee pot and mugs were on the table for them to get their own, and Fisher poured himself a mug, then added cream and some sugar to help get him going. He offered some to Reynard, who added cream to his.

"I called down to the fire station. They have the hotel parking lot open this morning, so you should be able to get your car. The hotel is not habitable, and they are going to have to do repairs before it can reopen." Gran seemed to know everyone. She sipped some juice, narrowing her gaze at Reynard.

"I see. Thank you. I'll walk down and get my car after this delicious breakfast," he said and began eating slowly. "You have a lovely home, and I appreciate you letting me stay very much."

"I'm sure Fisher made sure you were very comfortable," Gran said, and Fisher nearly choked on his coffee as he wondered if Gran knew what they had done last night. He lowered his gaze and tried not to look at her. Reynard's expression was completely schooled, so Fisher had no idea what he was thinking, and he lowered his eyes again to finish his breakfast.

Fisher cleared the dishes when they were done and offered Reynard a ride to the hotel before he went to work.

"I'll just walk. I need the chance to think," Reynard said, and after thanking Gran again, he got his bag, and Fisher saw him to the front door. "Thank you again… for everything." Reynard smiled and waved to Gran before leaving the house, tossing the bag over his shoulder as he headed down the walk.

Fisher closed the door and turned around.

"I need coffee and a nap. You and that boy kept me up half the night." Gran went back toward the kitchen, and Fisher couldn't help rolling his eyes before looking to heaven for help.

"You aren't mad?" he asked.

"Why? You think you invented sex? Gramps and I used to scorch the sheets when we were your age. How do you think I had six children—grew them in the garden?" She shook her head.

"Six?" Fisher asked. "But…." The math didn't add up.

She sat down. "I lost a girl and a set of twins. It happens to a lot of women."

He sat next to her. "I didn't know," he said softly, taking her hand.

She patted his. "But the loss didn't stop Gramps and me from trying. It was a long time ago, and I got three daughters in the end. They all made me happy, and that's all that matters." She turned to him. "And you make me happy, always have. So just be yourself." She leaned closer. "Still, for two men trying to be quiet, you two sure made a lot of noise. And for God's sake, the next time you bring a boy home, use the guest room. It's the one not right over my bed." She wiggled her eyebrows, and Fisher wished the earth would swallow him whole.

Fisher groaned and shook his head. "I can't believe we're having this conversation."

"Well, we are. So build a bridge and get over it." She kissed his cheek. "And know that I love you no matter what and that you can bring home anyone you love and I will support you." She squeezed his hand, and Fisher swallowed around the grapefruit that had formed in his throat.

"I thought you would have a problem with… well, me seeing men. I know we had the gay conversation a long time ago, but knowing and seeing are…."

She rolled her eyes. "I saw plenty when you were dating David, and I wish I had said something then. He was selfish and awful. You deserve to be happy. So find someone who makes you truly happy, and I'll be there the whole way." She sat up straight. "Now, you need to go to work, and I have to finish this and get something done before the caffeine wears off." She pushed back her chair and stood, heading outside, while Fisher went upstairs to get ready for work. He had a full day of traffic duty ahead, so before he left the house, he filled a travel mug with coffee to keep him company.

THE TOWN was charming, and Reynard figured he'd look around before leaving and continuing on his way. No one knew who he was, and he should be able to take a few hours to do ordinary things like check out the antique store or the other shops.

The lady in the artisan shop seemed really nice, and she liked to talk, which was great because Reynard liked her stories about how the town used to be. She even had pictures in her store. He liked that at the moment, she treated like him a regular person. At home, a simple conversation with her would be impossible.

She'd be nervous, and there would be no way either of them could just be this relaxed and… well… normal.

Two men came in the store and watched him for a few seconds. At least Reynard thought they might be watching him. He wasn't sure and didn't make eye contact. "Do you know them?" the nice lady asked.

Reynard shook his head. "No." Even as he answered, he could feel their gazes on him. He glanced to where they were shopping toward the back of the store. He thanked the lady for all her help and quickly left, heading down to the square before turning west, where he found a bookstore. Reynard went inside intending to find something to read, but as he browsed, the two men passed the store and then returned a few seconds later, looking at him through the window. His heart beat a mile a minute. At home he'd have people to handle situations like this, but here he was on his own. For a second he wished Louis was here.

He had no idea what these men wanted or who they were, but he had no intention of finding out.

An elderly gentleman sat behind the counter. "Is there a restroom?" Reynard asked as he paid cash for his books.

"Yes. Just toward the back." He smiled and gave Reynard his change.

Reynard thanked him and headed to the restroom, thankful there was a hallway and a back entrance. He opened the restroom door, blocking any view. Then he gently pushed the door closed, hurried the few steps down the hall, and went out the back door. Shit, he had no idea if these men were after him or what. They didn't have cameras or anything, but that didn't mean they wouldn't be waiting with them when he got out.

He managed to get across the parking lot and down the back alley, but as soon as he turned, he saw the men out on the sidewalk. He backed away and hurried back the way he'd come, continuing west until he entered a college campus where a myriad of people seemed to be heading to class. Reynard joined the flow, crossed the street, and wondered what the heck he was going to do.

FISHER'S DAY was busy. Every ridiculous speeding driver seemed to have decided that I-81 was some kind of drag strip. Fortunately, the stops were largely routine and normal. He handed out plenty of tickets and helped a vacationing couple with a flat tire.

"Gran?" he called after he'd changed clothes and returned to the house.

"I'm around back," she answered. He could have guessed. The temperature wasn't too warm, so she was going to be out in her garden. It was her happy place. "Bring some iced tea."

He stopped at the fridge to grab the pitcher and a couple of glasses, then took them out back. "It's lovely." He poured a glass and handed it to her. She got up from where she was kneeling on a pad. "You need to let me help you."

"I'm not ready for the cemetery yet." That was her usual response. To Gran, not being able to garden was the same as being dead. She took the glass once she was on her feet, and Fisher got a chair and placed it in the shade for her. Then he got a second for himself. "Everything is pretty."

"It is. You've done so much," he told her, sipping his own tea. "Work was good today, if a little tedious." Not every day could be like yesterday, thank goodness.

Gran drank her tea and sighed. "I'm going to need to make you dinner soon."

"I ordered a pizza on my way home. It should be here in half an hour." He sat back. "I even had them put pineapple on yours." Gran loved Hawaiian pizza, though he had no idea why. "So relax a little while." He worried about her, but Gran would just get upset if he said anything, so he kept quiet and did things for her when he could.

"Did you talk to our guest today?" Gran asked.

Fisher shrugged. "No. I didn't expect I would."

"But you liked him? And judging by the cries from last night, he liked you." Damn that knowing smile of hers.

"He's leaving town, and we both knew what it was. It's okay. I really wasn't expecting to hear anything. He was able to get the car and is probably hundreds of miles from here." That was how things worked, and railing against it did no good. If you spit in one hand and put wishes in the other, he knew which one held more… and was yuckier as well. Maybe not the best image, but what the hell.

He finished his tea and refilled their glasses and just sat with Gran for a while. The doorbell rang, and Fisher grabbed his wallet to pay the pizza guy.

Fisher opened the door to find Reynard on the front steps, a wild look in his eyes. The bag sat near his feet. He looked over his shoulder and then turned back to Fisher. "I need help, and I don't know who else to ask."

CHAPTER 5

REYNARD WASN'T disappointed to see Fisher again, but he wished it was under better circumstances. "Is this a police matter?" Fisher asked. "Because if it is, then you should call it in. I'm a state trooper. The borough police handle matters here."

"I don't know," Reynard answered, looking back over his shoulder again. God, he hated being this afraid. He kept expecting to see people following him… again. "Really, I don't."

"Okay." Fisher opened the door farther to allow him inside as a car pulled up in front. Reynard tensed, ready for action, but then a man hurried up to the door carrying two pizza boxes. Reynard breathed a sigh of relief as Fisher took them and paid the guy. Then he closed the door behind them, and Reynard felt safe for the first time in hours.

"Let me take Gran her pizza, and then you and I can talk." Fisher checked the top box, set the other on the table, and took Gran's outside. He returned a few minutes later. "Come on in. Gran wants to sit outside for a while."

"Thank you." Reynard slumped into one of the chairs, then sat up straight and rigid, his training kicking in. God, his mother would chastise him if she saw him slouch in a chair, no matter the reason. Fisher got two plates and poured him a glass of something.

Reynard took a sip, recognizing the American classic iced tea. He didn't care for it but drank it anyway.

"What's going on?" Fisher asked as he took a slice of pizza and offered one to Reynard.

Reynard hesitated. He had spent the past hour after evading the men he thought were watching him wandering through stores downtown and then in the woods in the back of a park, waiting to see if the men returned. It had taken a while for him to decide to talk to Fisher, but he still wasn't sure what to tell him. "I thought about leaving town this morning, but I figured I'd look around first. It's a charming place. I was doing a little shopping when I saw this man watching me. I didn't think too much of it. But when I moved to the next store, he was there when I came out of one of the rooms toward the back." Reynard tried to calm his racing heart.

"He may have been shopping," Fisher noted.

Reynard shook his head. "He was holding the merchandise but looking at me." He had seen that before every time he tried to shop on his own back home. Customers would stop and watch, and store owners sometimes tried to take pictures they could use to show that one of the princes shopped in their store. But Reynard didn't want to give up his cover—not unless he had to. As soon as anyone found out who he was, they started treating him differently and everything went to hell. Reynard just wanted to be himself, not the prince of Veronia, for once. Maybe that was too much to ask for, but he wanted to try.

"Okay." Fisher leaned forward. "You're going to have to give me a little more. Yeah, you're a hot guy, but that doesn't seem like a reason why someone would follow you around."

Reynard shrugged. "I don't know. That's why I came to you. Something is going on, and I have no idea what." As far as he could tell, he hadn't been recognized, and the man wasn't part of a security detail. He didn't have that look. If his family had sent someone to find him, it would be someone Reynard knew so he wouldn't panic the way he was doing now. Besides, if he *had* recognized him, then it would be all over the internet by now. He had checked, though, and saw nothing—not even a peep about his disappearance or the events he'd blown off. Silence. This was different from the tabloids or even what his family would do.

"Okay. So you think someone was following you, but you don't know why and you have no idea what they want. Did you try going up to the guy and asking him?" Fisher asked after swallowing a bite of the pizza.

"Is that some kind of American humor?" Reynard asked.

Fisher shrugged. "No, but maybe American directness. You may have looked like his brother-in-law or something. I don't know." He set down his food. "Let's look at what we know. You got here yesterday because your car broke down on a road trip, you weren't planning to be here, and now you think you're being followed." When Fisher said it that way, it seemed kind of dumb. Reynard might have let it go, but he'd seen the way that man had looked at him, eyes hard as stone and dark as the pits of hell. It had scared the crap out of him.

"I know it sounds crazy and doesn't make sense, but I saw the same man after I left the stores at the park over by the mansion. I drove there because I saw it on my GPS. I figured I was being paranoid, but another car pulled into the lot behind me, and I swear it was him. After that, I went over to the park near your house, parked the car, grabbed my stuff, and took off toward the back. I watched from the woods to see if he followed and then walked here."

"Did you see him?"

"No. But maybe he's waiting by the car or something, hoping I'll come back. I didn't know what else to do." Once again he thought about calling Louis or Langley to let them know where he was, but he didn't want his chance at a little freedom to be over. He was starting to understand just how much protection and security the people around his family provided them all, though. "So I came here." He began to think that he had imagined the whole thing.

Reynard had turned on the burner phone he'd used to message Louis, and there had been a couple of messages asking if he was okay and one to say that Langley was fit to be tied. That one had ended with a smiley face. There was definitely no love lost between those two. He had sent a text that he was okay and received an answer, but nothing more. Presumably Langley hadn't called in the troops yet or Louis would have mentioned it. He had been tempted to tell Louis where he was, but he held off. Maybe that was the bad decision, but he'd only been gone a day… a single day.

"Okay. Let's finish eating, and then I'll drive you back to get your car. If there's someone watching, they can deal with me and we'll see what they're up to." Fisher sounded confident, and Reynard ate a few bites of pizza. It was good, though very different from what he got when he was in Italy. But he had to admit, American pizza was definitely tasty.

"I see you turned up again," Gran said when she came inside. It took a second to read her expression, and Reynard wondered if he had made the right decision coming here. But then she smiled, and Reynard realized it was just her sense of humor. "I thought you were moving on."

"Change of plans," Fisher told her. "The hotels are still full with the car show, so Reynard is going to stay another night. He has an issue that I'm going to look into." Fisher stood and offered Gran his seat before taking care of his dishes. Reynard finished the last of his pizza and tea before joining him at the sink.

They might as well get this over with. Reynard wasn't sure if he hoped the car would be sitting there with no one around it, or if Fisher would find the man following him and get some answers.

"IS THAT the car?" Fisher asked as they pulled into the park drive just before dark. It was the only car in the lot, and the park seemed deserted.

"Yes." Reynard looked around for any sign of anyone at all. All he saw were the ducks and geese by the creek that ran through the west side of the park. "I don't see anyone."

Fisher got out and went over to the car, looking in the windows as he walked all around it. Only then did Reynard get out and unlock the doors using the key fob. Once again Fisher checked all around before getting into his own car. "Follow me back, and we'll put the car in the garage for the night."

Reynard nodded and started the engine. It purred to life, and he put it into Reverse and followed Fisher out of the lot and out to the street. Maybe he had been imagining everything. After all, there was no way anyone could have followed him. The car was a rental, and his money was untraceable. No one knew about his credit card. It also wasn't as though people were likely to recognize him. No, he should be fine, and if someone had taken an interest in him, then maybe Fisher was right and it was just a coincidence that they were in the same stores as him. Louis had the phone number he was using, and if he really needed to get in touch, he'd send a message.

On top of that, he was staying with a police officer. If someone was stalking him, that alone should give them pause.

Reynard turned left out of the park drive, heading toward Fisher's and his gran's. He hated being this nervous. Part of why he had wanted to be on his own was so that he could simply be himself and have some time as just Reynard and not a prince. He had hoped he could leave all this behind, and yet at the first hint of trouble, he had damn near panicked.

When he reached the house, Reynard pulled in through the open garage door and glided to a stop, then turned off the engine. After getting out, he closed the car door and leaned against it.

"Fisher," he said softly, trying to frame the question so he didn't give away how much he knew about what he wanted to ask. "I know you think I'm overreacting…."

"I never said that. Maybe you're getting yourself a little spooked. People do that when they're away from home and on their own. It happens."

Reynard let that go. He hadn't told Fisher that he had been on his own in some form or another since he was twelve years old and his father sent him to boarding school.

"Okay. But let's say that I was being followed and that I got away. The car was in the lot for a few hours.

What if they put a tracker on it?" All of the vehicles in the royal collection had trackers in case one of them was ever stolen or hijacked. It was one of the reasons why he never took a car whenever he snuck out—too easy to follow the trail.

Fisher didn't seem convinced, but he lay down and looked under the back of the car and then the driver's side before checking the front and then the passenger side. After a few minutes, Fisher stood, holding a small device in his hand. "Okay, I think you and I need to talk." He turned and left the garage.

Reynard had never thought of himself as a coward or someone who took the easy path. He knew he needed to stand up for what he believed in. His opinions differed from those of his father and brother. They were traditionalists, and Reynard felt the family and the country needed to move with the times rather than get stuck in the past. He never backed down from those views, at least in private, regardless of how his parents lectured him about a united front. What they really wanted was for him to see everything the way they did. Reynard tried new things and wanted to make his own way in the world when it would be easy to ride his family's coattails, the way second royal sons often did. Reynard wanted more, though, and he was willing and eager to go looking for it.

But in this moment, the urge to run and hide was nearly overwhelming. It wasn't so much telling Fisher who he was, but knowing that Fisher and Gran would look at him differently and act differently. He didn't want that. For a few hours, he had been just another person, and he liked it.

Finally Reynard squared his shoulders and left the garage. He closed the door and went to where Fisher sat in one of Gran's lawn chairs, staring in his direction with that same look he'd had when he pulled Reynard over. The cop was in the house, and Reynard knew all he could do was face the music.

"Okay," Reynard said, sitting in the other chair while Fisher stared at the tiny tracking device. "What do you want to know?"

Fisher leaned forward. "Everything." He showed Reynard the small black magnetic device. "Let's start with why someone would put this on your car."

Reynard nodded. "Shouldn't we get rid of it before whoever put it on the car shows up here?"

"I want some answers first," Fisher said without raising his voice, but the power behind it was unmistakable. Reynard's father spoke the same way. He never shouted or yelled, because he never had to. The authority in his voice said more than enough.

Reynard couldn't help staring at the device that meant the end of his trip and a return to his gilded cage. Eventually he would have had to go back, but this had come too soon. He shook his head. "Let's take care of that, and then I'll tell you everything."

Fisher watched him for a few seconds and then stood before going to the back door. "Gran, Reynard and I are going out for a few minutes. We won't be gone long." He then closed the door, and Reynard followed Fisher to his truck. They pulled away and out toward Hanover Street, then went south toward the freeway. Fisher pulled into the Five Guys parking lot and grabbed the device, stepped out, and walked toward the line of cars and trucks stopped at the light.

With a quick movement, he attached the tracker to the rear of a semi with its right blinker on to turn onto the highway going south. "It's going to take whoever did this a while before they figure out you haven't continued with your road trip." He backed away, and the truck moved forward, got on the highway, and picked up speed.

Reynard waited for Fisher, who climbed in and started the engine. "Now tell me what's going on. Why is someone tracking you?"

"I don't know," Reynard answered. "Not specifically. No one is supposed to know that I'm here."

Fisher narrowed his gaze. "So help me God, if I gave aid and comfort to someone on the run from the law, I will find you if you run and beat the crap out of you. Even after last night... I—"

Reynard put up his hands. "I'm not a criminal, and the law isn't after me. At least not the law of this country. Well, not even the one of my own, technically."

"*Technically*? What the hell does that mean?" Fisher put the truck in gear. "You better come clean and tell me the truth or else I'll take you to the station for suspicion of something, anything... and you can explain what is going on to them."

Reynard figured that was a bluff, but he decided not to call Fisher on it.

"As for who might be tracking me, I really don't know, but it probably has to do with the fact that I'm Franz Reynard Phillipe Henri San Luis, Prince of Veronia."

Fisher jammed on the brakes, sending them and the truck to an immediate halt. He was gaping like he had just seen a green space alien. His mouth worked, but nothing came out, and Reynard wondered what he was in for next.

CHAPTER 6

"You're *WHAT*? No fucking way. I ran a report on you when I pulled you over." Jesus, this was one hell of a kettle of fish. Not only had he pulled the guy over, but he'd taken a fucking prince home to stay at his gran's. What the hell? He didn't even want to *think* about the stuff they had done in his room.

"Yeah. And I gave you my international driver's license, which no doubt showed a diplomatic status, but that's all. It's done that way for our safety. But yeah, I'm the second son of King Henri San Luis of Veronia. My older brother, Albert, is the heir and crown prince. I'm the spare. If anything should happen to Albert, then I'm supposed to be ready to step in to take his place." Reynard rolled his eyes like it was some kind of joke.

Fisher didn't know where to start, but he was glad he was in the truck rather than at home, where Gran could overhear this.

A horn sounded behind him, and he pulled into a parking spot. "I need to know everything. If you lie to me again or leave shit out, I'll take you back to your damned car and you can ride off on your own."

"I never lied to you. Everything I told you about myself was true. I just left out the prince part."

"Why?" Fisher asked. He was trying to get his head around the fact that Reynard was royalty and that Gran had fed him corn pudding and chicken for dinner. God, he must have thought they were really dumb. Fisher hated that someone could have made a fool out of him and Gran.

Reynard shifted in his seat. "Do you know what it's like to be watched all day long? There are people who wake me up every morning by coming into my room to open the curtains. I can barely go to the bathroom alone. Then there's the endless parade of scheduled events, because that's what my family needs me to do. You got to pick your job. I didn't. I have to do what I was born into—period. So early yesterday morning, I snuck out. A friend helped me rent the car, and I have a credit card that no one knows about."

Fisher tried to take this in. "So you decided to take a break and have some fun."

"I wanted to see some things and spend some time on my own. I wanted to be just like everyone else and not be Prince of Veronia for a while. Everyone treats me differently." He sighed, and Fisher admitted to himself that he could understand that. "Think about it. If your grandmother had known I was a prince, would she have heated up some dinner? Or would she have insisted on cooking something special? And before you answer, her dinner last night was better than most of the 'special' food I've ever had."

"Okay. Gran would probably have… I don't know…."

"And you? How would you have treated me last night when I was standing outside the hotel? I'm willing to bet that someone would have seen to it that a hotel room was made available, and I would have been whisked away, leaving someone else out in the cold." Fisher had never thought of that. "Instead, I was the last one, and everyone else got the rooms that were available. I was going to be okay. I could have called someone, and they would have raced over to take me home. But this nice man offered me a place to stay. That would never happen to Prince Franz of Veronia. But to Reynard…."

Fisher nodded. "Okay, I get that. But you could have said something." He hated being lied to, and this felt like that. "I would have kept your secret, and I think you know that."

"It wasn't just about the secret. It's the way I'm treated. Even now, you're acting differently. Your speech is more formal, and you're looking at me like I'm a different species or something."

Fisher sort of smiled and felt his cheeks heat. "Actually, I was thinking of all the things we did last night. And that I did them to royalty. Say, if we did that in your country, could it land me in the dungeon?" Fisher thought he was being clever, but Reynard's scowl showed him his little joke had landed with a thud.

"Okay. You fucked a prince. What are you going to do? Call one of the tabloids to sell your story?" His scowl intensified.

Fisher gasped. "I was just making a joke. Did someone do that to you?"

"Which time?" Reynard asked bitterly.

Fisher shook his head. "Holy crap. What kind of people have you been dating?" He found that hard to believe. So Reynard hadn't told him he was a prince, but Fisher wasn't going to go running out to see how much money he could make. That was disgusting. "And before you say anything more, I would never do that kind of thing. What we did last night was private." Fisher tried not to be embarrassed. He had thought that Reynard would be gone and had let himself go in a way he wouldn't normally have. But he didn't expect to see Reynard again, and now, well…. The more he thought about it, the more he told himself he had nothing to be embarrassed about. He'd just been a little demanding and gotten controlling with a prince… for God's sake.

"Not everyone thinks that," Reynard said. "Most of the time, my life is fodder for newspapers, bloggers, and TikTok commentors. If I wear red, then it makes someone happy, and someone else gets pissed because their favorite color is blue and red makes them look puffy. There's a video out there if you want to look for it." He rolled his eyes. "Everyone watches the things I do all the time. I just wanted to get away from my life for a little while. I wasn't expecting to be tailed and stuff."

"Maybe it was someone looking to get a story?" Fisher offered.

Reynard shook his head. "If that were the case, they could have posted pictures of me coming out of your house with some sensationalist story about me staying with you last night. Nothing has been posted."

"And you're sure it isn't someone from your family?" Fisher had no idea what to do in this situation. There was a great potential for a lot of moving pieces. "Maybe someone was trying to keep tabs on you to keep you safe. Maybe they let you go because they had eyes on you the entire time." That seemed like a reasonable explanation.

"I left my phone back in New York and picked up a prepaid one. Louis, a friend of mine, has the number. He would have messaged me if the family had done something like that. I texted him this morning that I was safe, and when I turned on the phone before I came back here, there was a message saying that Langley was freaking out and getting ready to tell my father that I had taken off."

Fisher started to feel weird and didn't like the fact that they were sitting in an open parking lot, so he put the truck into gear and drove back toward home. "Okay. So it's not your family." Could someone else have followed Reynard? He wound his way back to the house, checking behind in case they were being followed. They weren't, as far as he could tell. Fisher parked on the verge outside the garage, and then they went into the yard. "I keep thinking about who could be after you, but I don't know enough to really be able to help."

"I was going to check social media once more to see if anything has been posted."

"And I'll check the police boards to see if any sort of report has been made regarding your disappearance, though that's unlikely. Your family may not be happy about it, but you haven't done anything illegal." Fisher went inside and got his laptop to log into the systems at work. He did a few searches and came up with nothing. There were no reports or complaints as far as he could tell. "Huh," he said once he checked locally. "The fire at the hotel is being investigated as intentional."

Reynard paled. "What if someone is after me?"

"And they set the hotel on fire? Why? To get you to come home with me?" Fisher shrugged. "This happens when a fire is complex. No determination has been made. That sort of ruling only means they don't have a clear cause and are looking deeper." He exited the system and passed the laptop to Reynard.

He set it on his lap and began typing. "I've gotten good at looking for recent stories and posts."

"I bet." Fisher sat back and put his feet up on one of the other chairs, trying to relax, but his mind kept coming back to the fact that Reynard was a fucking prince. He was used to all the best things that life could bring, and Fisher was just a cop from central PA. "Anything?"

"No. I'm checking things back home to see if there's anything posted." Reynard brought up some pages, and Fisher peered over his shoulder, but everything was in French, so he sat back and let Reynard do his thing.

"Why couldn't it be your family?" Fisher wondered if someone else could have followed Reynard.

"It's just not the way they do things," Reynard said definitively.

Fisher nodded, still running all this through his mind. "Who is Langley?"

"My assistant and secretary. He keeps my calendar and makes sure I get where I need to be on time. He also acts as my valet. He takes care of my clothes and uniforms… things like that."

Fisher kept himself from whistling. Reynard's world was so different from his, he was having a hard time wrapping his mind around it. "And you want to get away from a life where you have people to help you with the mundane aspects of life so you can be productive?"

Reynard leaned forward. "It's more than that." He seemed to be searching for what he wanted to say, and Fisher remained quiet, watching him. As concerned as he was for what was happening, that didn't stop his gaze from wandering over Reynard and his mind from recalling the view from the night before. Excitement built for a few seconds, because damn, Reynard was amazing in bed.

Reality burst his little fantasy bubble once Reynard began speaking. "I don't want to come off as some whiny rich kid who's unhappy with his life, because I'm lucky and I know it. Material things were never an issue, and I spend a lot of my time and efforts in Veronia working for people less fortunate. And it's those times, when I get to be myself, that I love the most. But it's not enough to be myself part-time."

"Explain this to me, because from where I'm sitting it sounds like you have a pretty sweet deal." It was difficult for Fisher to understand. "Gran and Gramps never had a lot, and neither did my parents. There were times when it was really hard for all of us. As in eating noodles and soup every day for a week or wearing my clothes until they practically fell off my back. You never had to worry about that, so please try to help me understand." Fisher didn't want to sound like a dick, but....

"Okay. Yeah, I didn't have to worry about that sort of thing. And people listen to me. But I don't have any kind of private life. I think I told you I wake up in the morning with someone coming into my room to open the curtains. There are people who clean my rooms for me. I have nothing private... if you know what I mean. Do you know what it feels like to have the head of housekeeping speak to your parents about certain items she found in your room?" Reynard's cheeks reddened, and damned if that look wasn't amazing on him.

"I didn't get to choose what I studied in school. The government and my father's advisors decided what I should study because it would be best for the crown. It didn't matter that my brother was the heir. I wasn't given a choice." Reynard swallowed hard, his gaze intense. "The day I was supposed to get my degree, there was a festival in Veronita, the capital. It's our independence day, and it's a huge deal. I wasn't able to attend the graduation ceremony like everyone else because the prime minister decided that the entire royal family should be at the festival as a show of unity and continuity." Disappointment rang in his voice. "My father agreed, and that was that. To make matters worse, I had to smile and wave in the royal parade and pretend that nothing was wrong. My entire life has been like that. Everything is out of my control." He sounded almost frantic. "All I wanted when I took off was a week or so of being able to live my own life and make my own decisions."

That was something Fisher *could* understand. "Sometimes family duty is hard. After Gramps died and Gran started to slow down…." A lump formed in his throat as the thought of the last of his family getting older and eventually leaving him hit hard, like it always did. He was a police officer, and he saw difficult situations on a regular basis. He had to be strong and hard, even dispassionate, but thinking about losing Gran made him lose his chill in an instant.

"I know. Losing my grandmother was heartbreaking. She was the closest person in the world to me. And you're right, family duty is hard, especially when everything is phrased as doing your duty." He breathed deeply and sat back. "I won't walk away entirely, because I know there's a lot of good that I can do. But is a week or two on my own too much to ask?"

"Did you ask your family?"

"Yes, I did. I asked my father if I could have a few weeks at the end of this trip to go off by myself, and he said that wasn't possible. After the trip to New York, he wanted me back in Veronia so I could be in trade meetings with him and Albert. Like anyone cared. And even if he *could* give me some time, I would need to have my security detail with me. And nothing calls attention like going everywhere with two men in black shadowing you." Reynard stood. "I didn't count on someone being able to track me like this, though."

Fisher stood as well. "I think it could have been the credit card. Someone may have been plugged into your finances more closely than you thought. Don't use it for a while, and with the tracker off down I-81, we may have thrown them off your trail for a while. You can stay here for a few days."

"What about your grandmother?"

"We'll tell her that you're going to stay and keep who you are quiet. But I do have a condition. That if this escalates further, we call your people to come get you." Fisher didn't like that Reynard had been followed, but hopefully it would be some time before whoever it was figured out the ruse, and by then Reynard could be any-where… at least as far as they knew. Fisher thought that whoever followed Reynard would indeed determine out that their tracker had been found, but he hoped the last thing they would think he would do was to stay put.

THE SUN set around them as he and Reynard sat on the patio, the stars coming out as darkness settled around them. Reynard had been jumpy for the past few hours, but he quieted, and his leg had stopped bouncing an hour ago. Fisher had a ton of questions, but he didn't want to ask them… not now. Reynard turned his face upward, looking at the sky.

"Come on," Fisher said, getting up. "Let's go." He motioned Reynard out the garden gate and to the truck. He waited for Reynard to get in and then pulled away from the garage.

"Where are we going?" Reynard asked.

"To the country," Fisher answered as he headed out of town.

It didn't take long for the lights of Carlisle to fade into the distance, and the night around them grew darker. Fisher pulled down a country road and then into a turnoff, doused the headlights, and cut the engine. They got out, and Fisher put down the tailgate as a seat. "Now you can see the stars," Fisher said.

The sky filled with lights, and as he looked up and points of reference faded away, the stars seemed to settle around him. "I used to want to be an astronomer," Reynard whispered, his hand brushing Fisher's leg, sending a zing of heat racing up his thigh. "Right there is Cassiopeia, a queen of myth. And the big dipper. In the winter, there's Orion. I always pictured him as a hunky, muscular kind of guy with a loincloth or something." He bumped Fisher's shoulder "Sort of like you."

"I don't think I've ever worn a loincloth," Fisher quipped to hide that he was flattered. As a kid, he had been small and picked on in school. Bullies had lined up to give him a hard time. He had been called names, and…. He pushed that out of his mind. Fisher wasn't that person any longer. As a teenager, he had grown tall and broad. Hours in gyms and a ton of exercise and training had left the guy bullies picked on far in the distance.

"Why not? You'd make an amazing Tarzan." Reynard grinned, his eyes sparking in the starlight. He licked his lips, and Fisher found himself doing the same, his belly filling with butterflies. Fisher closed his eyes, inhaling Reynard's rich scent, which called to him. Slowly, Fisher rolled his face to Reynard's direction, watching as his chest rose and fell. He licked his lips once again while his fingers brushed past Reynard's, sending a ripple of desire racing through him.

It took all of Fisher's willpower to stay still and not make a move. Oh, he wanted to, badly. Hell, every cell in his body called out for a repeat of last night out here under the stars, but that couldn't happen.

"Fisher," Reynard breathed, his voice deep, drawing at Fisher, threatening to tear down the last walls of his resistance. He swallowed hard. Reynard pulled at him. Even the way he said his name drew Fisher closer.

"It wasn't supposed to be this way. You were going to leave… and you will have to go soon." The words sent an ache through Fisher. "I thought last night was going to be it."

"Oh," Reynard breathed. "I shouldn't have come back."

"No. It's okay. You were in trouble." He was really messing this up. "I thought that after last night you were going to leave, so I sort of let myself go with you." It wasn't often he let his guard down and showed who he really was. Maybe that was a holdover from being bullied. He tended to keep his feelings to himself. That way it was safe.

Reynard turned to him. "I know you did. I felt it." He slipped his fingers between Fisher's. "Not many people show me anything about themselves, because I don't either. I'm not supposed to." They turned their heads, looking up at the sky once more, but Fisher's attention centered on the way Reynard held his hand. "We're supposed to put on a public face. The parliament and prime minister run the country. My father is the head of state. We give speeches and make public appearances, do charitable work, and provide a public face to the country and its people. Politics is something we stay out of because we can't appear to take sides.

My father thinks that means we show the world a smile and little else." The hurt in his voice filled the darkness.

"So you really can't be yourself," Fisher said, finally starting to understand.

"Yeah. And then last night I felt you. There was something honest and tender, yet strong about you. I knew that was the real you, and I opened up too." Reynard drew closer. "I never let anyone see who I am. That was drilled into me a long time ago."

Fisher turned toward Reynard. "And yet you let me see you."

Reynard closed the distance between them, his lips close enough that Fisher could feel his breath. "Yes, I did. You weren't alone last night. That was why it was so magical. Somehow, you and I, two people who are guarded, let ourselves be seen." Reynard stroked his warm hand over Fisher's cheek. "That isn't something to be afraid of but something to be thankful for." He drew closer into a kiss that built in intensity by the second.

Fisher couldn't deny him. He wound his arms around Reynard, returning the kiss, drawing him as close as he could. There was something about him that stopped Fisher's ability to think. All he wanted was Reynard, the scent of him, the way he felt in his arms, the sounds he made when they were together… and the trust in his eyes. "You are going to leave," Fisher said once Reynard pulled back. And maybe that was the hard part. "I was prepared for you to go in the morning. What I never expected was for you to return." And now that he had, Fisher wasn't quite sure what to do.

"I know," Reynard whispered. "I can't stay forever. Eventually I'll have to go home… return to being the puppet, the extra prince." He paused, and they turned back to the sky as a meteor streaked across the blackness. "I wasn't prepared for last night either."

Fisher swallowed, his mind racing. "Then what do we do?"

"You know the options as well as I do," Reynard said. "Tomorrow I can get in the car that's in your garage and head out. But I figure I may as well make the call and let Langley and Louis know where I am. They'll be here a few hours later, and I'll be on my way back to Veronia after that."

"What would you do?" Fisher asked. "Once you get home."

"Fall into the life my family wants me to have. I'll find a man that my family deems acceptable, and then that will be that. My brother will become king. I'll be the one they trot out on special occasions and for gay pride events. Other than that, I'll live the life of a largely unneeded royal. My family will expect me to be quiet, not make waves, and keep to myself."

"I see," Fisher said. "And what if you stay?" Just asking the question made his heart race and his mouth go dry. "What would be different? What could I possibly give you that you don't already have?"

Reynard sat up. "I honestly don't know. As soon as I make the call to let anyone know where I am, the wheels will start turning." Fisher sat up as well, looking deep into Reynard's eyes. "I can only hope that maybe I'll have something special to hold on to." He took Fisher's hands. "Will things be different? I really don't know. And yes, I will have to go back. I can't stay here forever. Someone will figure out who I am, and I can't stay away forever."

"So it's just a matter of *when*, not *if* you go back?" Fisher had known that was probably true.

"Yes." At least Reynard was honest. "I guess I was hoping that I could know what it truly felt like to have someone care about me for who I am." The heartache in Reynard's eyes drew Fisher forward, because he felt that was something everyone should know—even a prince.

CHAPTER 7

MAYBE REYNARD was simply asking too much of anyone. He was a prince, born into royalty, and maybe that was all that anyone would ever see in him. He could wish that people were different and that he could live the life he wanted, but he was coming to understand that maybe that was more than he had a right to expect.

Then Fisher leaned closer and kissed him, with "Reynard" on his lips. His name, not a title or some show of supposed respect. Instead, Fisher held him close, pummeling his lips with enough force to steal Reynard's breath.

At home no one touched him. It was tradition, and part of the mystique that since royalty was pre-ordained by God, they had some kind of divinity hanging over them and therefore they weren't to be touched. Fisher showed none of the compunction to stay away.

"Fisher," Reynard gasped as he sucked for air once his lungs had been kissed empty.

"Should I stop?" Fisher asked, and Reynard shook his head. "Good, because I see you. I don't know what you look like in all your princely finery, but I saw last night what you looked like without anything on, and no man can hide when he's laid bare." He held Reynard's gaze in his steely one. Damn, Reynard was coming to adore the hard edges of this man. He was so used to the people around him deferring to him, or people with all the roughness polished away. Fisher was nothing like that. He was real and a little hard, maybe even coarse… and perfect.

"And I see you. You know that." Everyone kept themselves guarded around him and his family. His father had always said that getting a true opinion was rarer than diamonds in a pigsty, and he was right. But somehow Reynard knew that with Fisher, he would get honestly and a real opinion when he needed it. That alone was sexy.

Fisher pulled back, both of them breathing deeply. Reynard's head seemed clouded, and his pants were two sizes too tight. He needed relief, and yet Fisher pulled away and sat back up.

"What are you doing?" Reynard asked, pulling him back.

"I'm not going to take you here," Fisher whispered. "The truck bed is rough, and I want to strip you bare and have you laid out in my bed, where I can have you all to myself." He leaned closer.

"And here I thought you brought me out here to seduce me," Reynard teased, unable to look away from Reynard.

"Oh, I don't know. I seem to remember you making remarks about loincloths, so maybe I'm the one being seduced." He slipped his fingers through Reynard's hair and held his head.

"It could be a mutual seduction," Reynard offered, quivering as Fisher popped open a couple of Reynard's shirt buttons and tweaked his nipple. Reynard whimpered from deep in his throat, and Fisher's cock throbbed in his jeans. Damn, Reynard could get him revved up faster than anyone he had ever met in his life. "I think we're past mutual at this point."

Fisher seemed to agree with that. Still, he pulled away before he ended up doing what he had said he wasn't going to do. Reynard was balanced on the edge of a knife, and it would only take a little nudge for him to pull Fisher on top of him.

Taking a deep breath, Fisher slid to the edge of the tailgate and climbed down, adjusting himself in his jeans while waiting for Reynard to climb off as well. After pushing the tailgate into position, Fisher got into the truck and seemed deep in concentration on driving back to the house.

"Why aren't you looking at me?" Reynard asked when they were about halfway there, wondering why Fisher was ignoring him.

"Because if I do, I'm likely to either drive off the road or pull to a stop and ravish you right here in the middle of the damned road." Reynard heard how growly he was, which only added to his own excitement. They increased speed, going faster until they reached the edge of town. "Now, I think you need to sit there and let me drive."

"And what about when we get to your grandmother's?" Reynard asked.

Fisher tensed slightly and growled once more. "You had to bring her up, didn't you?" Talk about a cold bucket of water. Reynard should have probably kept quiet. "The last thing I wanted to think about at this moment was my grandmother and how she's going to react to another night of our bedroom athletics. She's already amused by last night, and I hate the thought of her knowing what we were doing. It's private." The touch of American prudery was cute, and Reynard found the possessiveness touching.

"It got you thinking about something other than driving off the road, so yeah." Reynard sat back, grinning wickedly as Fisher concentrated more thoroughly on his driving.

"I could stop and kiss that grin of yours away. Hell, I could even get you revved up and then leave you hanging."

Reynard made an undignified noise. "You already did that." He sat back, and they slipped into silence, the tension in the cab building with each passing minute. The temperature rose even with the air-conditioning, and by the time they reached the house, he was pretty sure the cab of the truck made a school locker room smell like perfume.

Without a word, Fisher parked and followed Reynard into the house, then closed and locked the door. Reynard felt Fisher's gaze on him the entire time. His grandmother must have already been in bed, and after Fisher checked that her door was closed, he turned to Reynard. "You've got about thirty seconds to get up to my room or I'm going to fuck you wherever I catch you, Gran or not." He took a deep breath, but Reynard stood still, gaping. "I mean it. You need to move."

Reynard swallowed and took off up the stairs, knowing Fisher was watching every move.

"Even hurrying, you moved gracefully," Fisher whispered as he slowly ascended the stairs behind him. Reynard moved as quickly and quietly as he could, desperate to get to the bedroom.

Reynard pulled off his shirt as soon as he was inside the room, then toed off his shoes, climbed onto the bed, and lay back to slip out of his pants. He stopped when Fisher saw him, the intensity in his eyes nearly overwhelming, his hands holding the fabric but still.

Reynard couldn't move, the sight in front of him mesmerizing. Fisher was stunning, his lips slightly parted, shirt stretched over his chest. His muscled arms flexed slightly just from how Fisher held them. His eyes were dark and deep, lids hanging slightly closed in what Reynard interpreted as anticipation.

He licked his lips, swallowing to wet his dry throat. This was someone who instantly sent his heart racing and his temperature through the roof. For a second, Reynard thought about demurring and going to the bathroom to hide out. He wanted Fisher with everything he had, but what the hell was he going to do when he had to leave?

His mind played a mini tennis match for about three seconds, and then Fisher stepped forward into the room. Resisting him was useless. It wasn't like he made a conscious decision—his body and heart knew what they wanted, and they overruled the reluctance in his head with a wave of desire that crashed over everything else.

"Damn," Fisher sighed as he closed the bedroom door, sending a second wave of molten fire running through Reynard.

"Is this what you wanted back in the truck?" Reynard asked, shucking the last of his clothes before lying naked in Fisher's bed, cock straining to his belly button. He wanted him, and he loved how Fisher seemed taken with him, the man.

Fisher nodded. "Yeah, you drive me out of my mind."

"And it isn't because of who I am?" Reynard asked.

Fisher shook his head… and then seemed to change his mind and nodded. In an instant Reynard wondered if he had been reading Fisher all wrong. Reynard lowered his gaze to the bedding, feeling like a fool. "It is because I'm a prince."

"No." Fisher closed the distance between them, as if drawn to Reynard by some invisible force. "It's because you're smart and funny. Because you have a good heart, and because you're the hottest man I've ever seen." He climbed onto the bed and crawled up to Reynard before pressing him down against the mattress, taking his lips in a hard kiss that left them both shaking. If that was true, then who Reynard was might have drawn them together. And it was likely that who he was would pull them apart. It was inevitable and a fact of Reynard's life.

But Reynard didn't want to think about that. Not right now. He was too enthralled by how Fisher tasted and felt against him to worry about that. His firm lips and the fact that Fisher really knew how to kiss only drove Reynard's passion.

"Fisher… I…," Reynard gasped.

"What?" Fisher asked, his lips an inch from Reynard's. He carded fingers through his hair, keeping it out of his eyes. Reynard could lose himself in that touch.

"I don't want to hurt you."

"I know. But what can we do?" It seemed that Fisher could see what was coming as well.

Reynard wished he had the answer, but all he could do was remain silent. This had to be Fisher's decision. If he pulled away, Reynard wouldn't blame him.

Fisher paused and took a deep breath. "Gran told me when Grampy got sick that all we could do was take things one day at a time."

It was all that both of them could do. In a few seconds, what Reynard wanted crystalized in his mind.

"If we can do that, then the time we have together is special, and what might happen can stay in the future," Fisher said.

It seemed Fisher felt the same way. He knew he had no hold on Fisher, and it wasn't likely that he ever would or could. "I like that," Reynard whispered before kissing him hard, and within seconds it was all Reynard could do to think at all. Fortunately thinking was overrated, and at a moment like this when Reynard tugged at Fisher's shirt, baring his skin, silence was definitely golden.

FINALLY REYNARD managed to get Fisher naked and lying on the bed. Reynard straddled him, looking at the powerful man beneath him. He had no illusions that he was the one in charge. Fisher had made that clear last night, and it seemed from the burning and the strength in his touch that it was the same tonight. Not that Reynard minded in the least.

"You like that I'm strong?" Fisher asked, and Reynard nodded. "I'll never hurt you."

Reynard leaned forward. "I know that."

Fisher tugged him closer, taking his lips in a passionate kiss that left Reynard shaking.

"But I also know that you like to be the one calling the shots." He rolled his hips, sliding along Fisher's cock.

"And you're a tease," Fisher growled deeply.

"It's not teasing if I follow through, and I have every intention of doing just that." He smiled and loved how Fisher did the same back to him. Teasing, playing in bed… those were new sensations to him. Usually the guys he'd been with were interested in getting down to business, but Fisher held him and seemed intent on keeping the pace slow.

"It definitely is when you're acting like a minx." He kissed him, engulfing Reynard in his arms before rolling them on the bed until Reynard was under Fisher's solid weight. "Now that's so much better. I like having you under me." He shifted slightly. "I'm not too heavy, am I?"

"No." Fisher's weight was solid and comforting. Reynard liked it. "Most of my life is filled with protocol, yet even then I feel like I'm operating without a net most of the time, like everyone is just waiting for me to mess up. You're solid, and you make me feel cared for." Maybe that wasn't the exact word, but it worked. Fisher would see to it that nothing bad happened to him.

"That's not the way to live. And you don't have to worry about that here. I'll be your safety net." Before Reynard could respond, Fisher slid down his body, and all Reynard could do was moan softly as he blazed a trail with his tongue and lips to Reynard's cock, which he took deep and fast in a single movement, taking away his ability to talk.

Reynard held still, letting waves of passion and desire wash over him. He gripped the bedding as Fisher bobbed his head, sucking hard, pulling Reynard's hips off the bedding. Fisher slipped his hands under him and cupped his ass, lifting him slightly, taking away Reynard's ability to move. He was at Fisher's mercy… and there was nowhere else he wanted to be. While Fisher liked to be in charge, he also seemed to want to give as much as possible.

"Not going to last," Reynard whispered, and Fisher backed away. Reynard shook as Fisher lowered him to the bed, his hands exploring while Fisher kissed him hard.

Fisher gripped his cock, holding it tight without moving as he probed Reynard's lips with his tongue. "You are sexy as all hell."

Reynard held Fisher's gaze. "And you make me want to march into hell with you if this is what it feels like." At this moment, Reynard would follow Fisher anywhere. He groaned when Fisher released him, and when he sat up, the cool air-conditioned air kissed his skin. Fisher's weight shifted, and soon he was back. A *snick* told him that Fisher had the slick, and then a finger, followed by another, breached him.

"Are you ready for me?" Fisher asked, scissoring his fingers and driving Reynard crazy.

"I think I was born ready for you." God, Fisher made him feel things he never thought possible. He could be himself, and he didn't have to worry about Fisher thinking badly of him or running to the press with some lurid story.

"Me too." Fisher drew back and got himself ready before filling Reynard slowly, joining them together physically and looking deep into Reynard's eyes, carrying him away.

In a matter of minutes, Reynard was shown a completely new way of looking at his existence. Up until now, he had no idea that he could be this happy. His mind and spirit seemed to slip out of his body, traveling with Fisher. Then, as quickly as he'd slipped away, he slammed back into himself as Fisher took him on a journey that Reynard hoped above all hope would never end.

"Don't stop," he managed to croak, and Fisher leaned over him, pressing deep before driving him absolutely wild. "Please… I'll give you anything…."

Fisher drove harder, and the room spun as Reynard did his best not to scream at the top of his lungs as his release barreled into him at a hundred miles an hour. He held off completion as long as he could, with Fisher going still, and Reynard tumbled into near oblivion.

He lay unmoving, breathing deeply, holding Fisher as afterglow settled over them. He didn't want to move in case the spell that held him evaporated. The glow lasted until their bodies separated.

Reynard shivered, and Fisher left the bed, then returned quickly and slipped under the covers.

"I don't understand what happened," Reynard whispered. "I wasn't here for a while, and…." He tried to put his mind around it and failed.

"Why do you think people mix sex and drugs? They both feel good." Fisher tugged him closer. "And sometimes when sex is just right, it's like both of them at once."

Reynard snorted and covered his mouth. If anyone heard him make that sound, it would make the papers for sure… somehow. "You're telling me you're that good? Isn't that a little cocky?"

"Says the man who just lost himself for a while," Fisher whispered as he wrapped his arms around him, pulling Reynard against his warmth. "To be honest, it's never happened before. I only read once that it was possible." He snickered. "I'm pretty pleased that it happened for both of us."

Reynard rolled his eyes. "You seem a little too pleased with yourself." He snuggled closer. "But I'm not going to question it. The only thing I want to know is if I'm going to have to look at your grandmother across the breakfast table and have to explain to her why her precious grandson managed to take the two of us on a trip to heaven and back."

Fisher groaned. "She told me about the first time this morning, so yeah, she doesn't miss much. And I expect she'll be giving both of us the side eye.

"Great. Just great."

Fisher held him closer. "You have nothing to worry about. Gran may give us a hard time or ask us to keep it down, but she doesn't gossip, and she isn't going to go running to the press."

Reynard realized that Fisher had hit the nail on the head. His mind was still working the way it always had, and he needed to think differently around Fisher.

"Just relax and try to go to sleep. I checked outside to make sure there was no one hanging around." He tugged Reynard a little closer, and he closed his eyes, doing his best to try to sleep.

CHAPTER 8

FISHER GOT up early, letting Reynard sleep. He dressed and checked out front and did a walk out back by the garage like he had the past two quiet mornings, just to make sure that no one was hanging around. He'd spent a good part of the night once again wondering who could have been following Reynard. Despite what Reynard had told him about his family, they were still high on Fisher's list of suspects. But in case it wasn't them….

He went inside to find Gran at the kitchen table in her yellow robe. "I made coffee." She sipped from her mug, and Fisher poured himself some and joined her at the table. He sipped the wake-up juice, grateful for something to perk him up. "You and Reynard sure went at it last night… again."

He forced himself not to do a spit take, but he coughed anyway. As soon as Reynard had come to bed, it had been fireworks between them. Fisher just couldn't get enough of him, and it seemed the feeling was mutual.

"I'm just teasing you. I went right to sleep and didn't hear anything." Sometimes Gran was just wicked. "Have you really hit it off, or is this just a case of having the long-range hots for each other?" Her grin told him she was having too much fun with this.

"Doesn't matter." Fisher slumped slightly. "He's only staying for a few days, and then he'll have to go." He drank some more coffee and wondered why he didn't just tell her about Reynard. But he didn't know how Gran would react, and he didn't want to deal with the whole prince thing. Reynard was another guy, as far as he was concerned, and if he wanted to stay as anonymous as possible, then Fisher would abide by his wishes. Though he had no doubt Gran would be pissed at him once she found out.

She leaned closer, her gaze missing nothing. "The question is whether you want him to go. It seems to me you are getting yourself in deeper than you expected."

Fisher shrugged. "It's okay, Gran. I know what's happening, and I have it under control." Now, that was a lie and he knew it. The truth was that he *didn't* want Reynard to leave. He liked him, and they clicked. But facts were facts. Reynard couldn't just spend the rest of his life in small-town Pennsylvania. This was an interlude for him, a chance to sow his wild oats before he had to return home and face the life he was born into. Fisher knew in the long run that he had to simply let him go. They had talked about it, and he had his eyes open. It didn't mean it wasn't going to hurt.

Jesus, he was in real trouble if he was already worrying about how much he was going to miss Reynard after just two days. God, he had it bad, and he didn't know what the hell to do about it.

Gran huffed and didn't say anything more. She had more of her coffee, and Fisher finished his before heading upstairs to get dressed for work.

When he entered the room, Reynard was still asleep, spread out on the bed like the prince he was, taking all the space possible. The covers pooled around his waist, and it was so tempting to crawl back under the covers and give Reynard a wake-up call he wasn't likely to forget. Fisher's body thrummed at the thought, but after checking the time, he quietly went to his closet to get his uniform.

"Are you going to work?" Reynard asked, his voice heavy with sleep.

"Yes. I'm on shift in an hour." He had more traffic control duty, and that meant sitting in the patrol car in one of the partially hidden spots to watch for speeders. It wasn't particularly appealing, but it was important. Getting people to slow down meant fewer accidents to respond to, and that was always a good thing. "I'll be back a little after five." He leaned over Reynard and kissed him lightly.

"I should probably go. You don't need me staying here all day." Reynard sat up and groaned. "I don't have anywhere I need to be," he said quietly, almost to himself. "There's no calendar of events waiting for me, no list of places I have to go." He blinked and smiled. "It never occurred to me before, but the day is my own." He lowered his gaze. "And I don't have a clue what to do with it."

Fisher chuckled. "If you stay here, I'm sure Gran will be plenty happy to put you to work helping her. Growing up, Gran had no trouble finding me things to do."

"Are you sure it's okay for me to stay? I don't want to be a burden on you or your grandmother." There were those proper manners again.

"I'm sure. Gran spends a lot of her days alone, and I'm sure she'll appreciate the company. I need you to keep an eye out and call me if you think someone is hanging around. I'd like to catch up with them and get to the bottom of this." He kissed Reynard again and began changing.

He had his uniform on and was checking himself in the mirror when a firm knock on the door startled him. Reynard had already dressed, so he opened it to find Gran standing in the doorway, the cane she used for coming upstairs in her hand. She glared at both of them. From her expression, he half expected her to brandish the cane like a weapon.

Instead she held out her phone. "Would one of you like to explain why I have a lost prince in my house, who it seems a number of people are now looking for?" She dropped her phone into her pocket and put her hands on her hips.

Fisher knew that look, and they were in tee-rub-bull. Fisher knew this was his responsibility, and he was about to offer an explanation when Gran directed her ire at Reynard. "Young man, you really need to tell me what's going on and why you're here."

"He ran away for a while and ended up here," Fisher offered. "I didn't know at first, but Reynard told me yesterday."

"And neither of you thought of telling me?"

Man, he hated that look, like he was five years old and had been caught with his hand in the cookie jar.

"Why?" Fisher asked quickly. "Do you want to sell the story?" He was a little out of line, but he had to bring the seriousness home to Gran.

"Of course not," Gran snapped. "But I have a right to know who's staying in my house."

Fisher stared her down. "You already know him. He's Reynard, and he's been staying with us for a few days. He's a nice man, and you like him. That's all you really need to know."

Her gaze grew even more heated, and Fisher thought she might smack him on the bottom like she'd done when he was six. "You know what I mean."

"Gran… does it really matter?"

She rolled her eyes and turned to Reynard. "According to this article, your family is worried about you and thinks you may be held against your will."

Reynard shook his head. "That's just something the press have taken on themselves. One of my security men knows I'm okay because I have contacted him each day. So that's a bunch of crap."

"I see," Gran said. "Then…."

"All I wanted was some time to be myself. Everyone around me bows and scrapes all the time. I wanted to find people who could like me for me. Is that too much to ask for?"

Gran patted his shoulder. "If your family is behind this article, then maybe it is. It seems they are putting on the pressure. Fisher, you need to get yourself into work, and while you're at it, you might want to find out if anything official has been submitted."

"Shit," he muttered. He could always report that he had seen Reynard and that according to him, he was fine and not being coerced in any way, but that would give away Reynard's location and bring reporters and maybe even Reynard's family to town, which was more than any of them needed.

"Just go. Reynard and I will have a little talk while you're gone." She actually smiled, and Fisher kissed her cheek.

"Thanks, Gran." He did a final check on his uniform and then left the room, hurrying off to work so he could try to get a handle on what was happening.

TRAFFIC DUTY meant a lot of time by the side of the freeway. Fisher set his speed detection equipment along with the speed threshold and settled in to wait. His real purpose in being there was to slow folks down, and just the sight of his patrol car was usually enough.

How is it going? Wyatt messaged him through the system.

Fisher hesitated. He typed and deleted his response a couple of times before finally sending, *I need some advice.*

His phone rang almost immediately. "What's up?" Wyatt asked as soon as Fisher answered.

"I'm not sure how to ask. But do you remember that guy I stopped a few days ago with the diplomatic passport?"

"Yeah. I saw a story this morning. Can you believe it? You pulled over a prince for speeding. That's a story you can tell in the squad room until you retire." He seemed pleased. "I already reported that we pulled him over and that after having car trouble, he planned to leave town once he got a new rental car. I also reported that he was on his own and that at the time we saw him, he wasn't in any sort of distress and that he was alone."

"Is there some official reporting? Have they filed him as a missing person?" Fisher asked, knowing he needed to keep his questions within the realm of professionalism. "I was just about to check to see."

"Not yet. But I checked with the captain, and with the story hitting social media big-time, he asked me to contact the family and provide what little information we have. He said this morning to try to put their minds at ease about him being abducted and that we know nothing of his current whereabouts."

Fisher checked traffic, turned off his vehicle, and then stepped out of the car, disconnecting his phone from the vehicle's systems. "But what if I have information on his whereabouts?"

Wyatt paused. "Do you know where he is?"

"I might have an idea," he prevaricated.

Wyatt was quiet for a few seconds. "No official report has been made, so we aren't compelled to provide information. I was being helpful because the family put out a call requesting it. Do you know if he's okay?"

"Yes. He's fine, and he isn't being held against his will." Though Gran might be giving him an earful about now, so he might *wish* he had been kidnapped instead. Gran could be quite forceful. Still, he was pretty sure Reynard would turn on the charm and have Gran eating out of his hand.

"Then there isn't anything to report or tell anyone. He's a grown man, and he has a right to his own free will. And if he wants to spend some time away from his family, I can't blame him, especially if the attitude of the man I spoke with is any indication. Some hoity-toity guy named Langley or something." Fisher could almost see Wyatt rolling his eyes. "If I had to deal with a guy like him every day, I'd want to run away too."

Fisher felt better, but he wasn't sure how he felt about Wyatt letting this Langley guy know that Reynard had been in Carlisle. Hopefully they thought Reynard had left town and that would be the end of it. There had been no sign of anyone hanging around the house or looking for Reynard, and other than this family story, things had been quiet. But Fisher figured it was only a matter of time before Reynard's family turned up the heat. "Thanks." He got back into the car and started the engine, kicking on the air-conditioning to cool the inside the car, which had heated quickly in the summer sun.

"HOW WAS your day?" Gran asked as Fisher trudged through the back gate into the yard.

"Long," Fisher answered. He gave her a hug and then went inside to get out of his uniform and lock up his gun and equipment. Then he showered and changed before finding Reynard reading on the bed in the guest room.

"When is your next day off?" Reynard asked, looking bored out of his mind.

"Tomorrow. I have the entire day. Usually I take Gran to the store and things." He sat on the side of the bed and patted Reynard's leg. "But I could do that this evening. Did you have something in mind?"

"I don't know. I've been here for the past few days, and I wanted to have some fun. Maybe go out and do things normal people do."

Fisher shook his head. "What do you think our lives are like? That we have this well of fun that we don't share?" He caught Reynard's gaze. "This is it. You've seen my life. I go to work, come home, help Gran, go to bed, and do it all over again." His life was pretty boring—nothing like the one Reynard led most of the time. "I know you think that your life is suffocating, but try living ours. Money is a constant worry and struggle. I pay Gran rent so that she can stay in her house and not have to go into some assisted-living home. Her Social Security and the small pension she gets from Gramps isn't enough to keep the house going. You get to see the world, and I haven't taken a trip that was more than a few hours away by car in years." He needed Reynard to understand that maybe he didn't have it so bad.

Reynard sat up. "I'm sorry." He looked down for a few seconds and then raised his head with an excited grin. "Anyway, I was thinking that we could go to this chocolate place. There's a fun park with rides."

"Hershey Park?" Fisher asked. "Are you sure you want to do that? There will be tons of people around."

"And all of them going about their business of having fun. I haven't shaved in a few days, so I'm starting to look kind of scruffy." He ran his hands over his cheeks. Fisher had noticed, and as far as he was concerned, Reynard looked sexier by the day with his short, thick black beard. "Royal family members aren't allowed to have facial hair. It's tradition. And I can get a hat and sunglasses. No one is going to expect me to be there, and it isn't like they have roving reporters in the place."

Fisher couldn't argue with that. People tended to concentrate on themselves and didn't look too closely at others. "We could go, if you like. But we'd have to be prepared to leave if you were recognized."

"Other than the story put out by my parents, I'm not likely to be known outside of my area of the world. The European tabloids are interested in me, but my country is too small for me to be really famous. I'm not like William and Harry, who everyone knows. Thank goodness."

"Do you want to see about getting tickets?" Fisher got up and retrieved his laptop, returned, and handed it over to Reynard.

He typed and smiled. "Okay, I can get us tickets, and I can reserve a cabana near the pool. Do you think Gran would like to go? The cabana comes with an attendant, and she can get whatever she'd want to eat or drink."

Fisher doubted it, but he went downstairs and found her in the living room with her feet up. "Reynard and I are going to Hershey Park tomorrow."

"That's nice," she said with a smile.

"Do you want to go? He says he's reserving a cabana near the pool in the water park."

She thought for a minute and then shook her head. "You two youngsters go and have fun. I'm going to stay here. Some of the ladies in the garden club are going to lunch, and I think I'll join them." She returned to her reading, and Fisher relayed the message to Reynard, who went ahead and got their tickets.

"Do we need anything else? I got the line-hopper thing so we don't have to stand in long lines." He seemed really excited. "I also ordered hats, towels, drinks, and food to be delivered to the cabana." He set aside the computer. "The park opens at eleven."

"You're going to need a bathing suit," Fisher said.

"I have one in this bag somewhere." He grinned, and Fisher had to give the guy some credit. He really seemed to want to do this, and for the first time since they'd met, Fisher got a glimpse of the kind of kid Reynard might have been. It was good to see some of that enthusiasm, and Fisher had to admit it was catching. Maybe tomorrow would be a fun and uneventful day. Yet something prickled at the back of his mind, and he wished it would go away.

CHAPTER 9

THE CARS were lined up to get in, and Reynard was a little overwhelmed as they waited in traffic. This was something new for him. Back home, people parted and roads were blocked off so the royals could get where they needed to go. Here, he waited with everyone else until they parked, and then Fisher grabbed the backpack he'd put all their things in and they headed into a flow of people.

"Are they all going where we are?" He was a bit surprised at the sheer number of people.

"Yes." Fisher handed him sunglasses from the backpack, and Reynard put them on. "Are you a ride kind of guy?"

Reynard didn't know what to say. "You mean like a carousel?"

Fisher pointed. "No, like that." People screamed as a train went over the crest of a monster roller coaster and barreled toward the earth. "Candymonium is an amazing ride. I figure we'll go on that later and head toward the back of the park. There are more coasters and lots of other attractions."

Fisher used the tickets Reynard had gotten to get them inside, and they strode through the park to the cabana entrance. After checking in, they were shown their covered area with lounges, tables, and even a small bar with the drinks Reynard had arranged for.

"What about our things?"

"They'll watch everything so we can go off and ride whatever we want, then return for lunch and relax during the hottest part of the afternoon." Fisher took his hand and led him away. Together they were off.

"You have to be kidding me," Reynard said as Fisher got them in line for SkyRush. The thing was huge, and every trainload of people that went by screamed their lungs out.

"Come on. It's fun," Fisher told him as they reached the front of the line, and before Reynard knew it, they were being seated in the car.

"How fast does this thing go?"

"Only eighty miles an hour. Don't worry." That was faster than Reynard had been going when Fisher pulled him over. Fisher helped him get the harness bar over his shoulders and snapped into place. Then they were off and up the hill before barreling down the other side, screaming along the coaster track, and all Reynard could think was how his father would have man-eating puppies if he could see him at that moment. By the time he had a chance to be scared, they were pulling into the station.

"Well?" Fisher asked as they climbed out and were leaving the ride.

"Can we go again?" Reynard asked.

"As many times as you want, but look… there are half a dozen more." And with that they were off. Reynard wanted to do each and every one of them.

"I think I'm addicted to these things," Reynard told Fisher as they got in line for Great Bear, his heart still racing with excitement, and he wondered if it was from the coasters or the fact that he was doing this with Fisher.

IN THE heat of the afternoon, after eating, they lay on lounges in the shade of their cabana. Reynard closed his eyes and let his mind drift, listening to kids splashing and laughing in the nearby pool. Above all the noise, he remained aware of where Fisher was. All he had to do was stretch out his arm to touch Fisher, and he didn't have to see him to know where he was. It was like his body had Fisher radar.

Fisher's lounge creaked, and Reynard was about to sit up to see what he was doing when the light around him lessened. Fisher had to be closing the drapes along the sides of the cabana, darkening the space. "It's so warm," Reynard said as a breeze blew over him.

"I turned on the ceiling fan," he said softly and then sat back down. Reynard lay still and let himself doze for a while, just enjoying Fisher's company.

Reynard came to as cold slid up his arm. "What are you doing?"

"Waking you up," Fisher said, dropping the ice chip to the floor. "Do you want to ride some more?"

Reynard sat up, rubbing his eyes. "I was thinking we could go in the pool." He had been hearing everyone splashing around for a while, and it was still hot.

"Then let's change," Fisher said, and he grabbed the bag and led the way to one of the changing rooms.

The small cubicle had a bench and drying area. Reynard pulled off his clothes and searched for his suit in the backpack. Fisher's hands slid down his back, and Reynard stood upright. Fisher's arms encircled him, and he swallowed hard and closed his eyes as Fisher's hands roamed over his chest and belly. "You're so naughty," Reynard scolded without trying to move away. This felt so damn good.

"You know I could fuck you right here," Fisher whispered in his ear. Reynard lowered his gaze, cock pointing straight out. There was no way he could get his suit on and leave this room without flashing half the patrons of Hershey Park.

"You're going to have to do something." Fisher had him turned on in seconds, and Reynard wasn't going to leave this way. Thankfully Fisher slipped his hand lower and slid his fingers along the length of Reynard's cock.

He stifled a gasp and bit his lower lip to keep from crying out as Fisher stroked him harder with one hand, holding him tightly with the other as he sucked on Reynard's ear. Damn, it felt good, and as Fisher stroked him, tightening his hold, the sounds around them dissipated until it was just Fisher and him. It didn't matter that there were tons of people outside in the park. All that counted was Fisher and the way he made him feel. His entire body felt like it was on fire, and sweat broke out on his forehead as Fisher heightened the tension, lightly squeezing a nipple as he tugged harder and faster. "I know just how you like it now."

Reynard nodded, his legs and back growing tense as pressure and pleasure built by the second. He wanted this to last for hours, but his body had other ideas. He clamped his eyes closed and did his best to keep from crying out. Under most circumstances, it would be his own hand providing him with the relief, but with Fisher, Reynard had no control, and the uncertainty only added to the excitement. His breathing went ragged and shallow as Fisher sucked at the back of his neck.

"Tell me what you like," Fisher whispered.

"This… you… I…." His brain seemed to have switched off.

Fisher held him tighter, pinching his nipple just a little more, sending a jolt of almost pain racing through him. It was fantastic, and his right leg shook as Fisher stroked him harder and faster, driving Reynard out of his mind. "I know you're getting close. I want you to come for me. Can you do that?"

Reynard hummed a response.

"Okay, good. Now let go. I have you, and I'm not going let you fall. Just put yourself in my hands and fly." Fisher stroked hard, and Reynard tensed and stilled, unable to control his body as his release raced through him. He came hard, shaking as he painted Fisher's hand with his desire.

His knees felt like they were going to give out, but Fisher held him. Reynard found he couldn't move, and he breathed the sultry air deeply, trying to get enough oxygen into his lungs. Still, Fisher had him and didn't let him go until Reynard found his balance and shifted away from Fisher. He blinked and then slowly sat on the bench, breathing deeply, his head still light.

Fisher cleaned up the area with paper towel while Reynard got his suit on. Normally he would have worn a small skintight bathing suit, but Fisher had loaned him boardies that he said would probably be better for the park. It still took Reynard longer than it should have to get them on because he kept getting distracted by the sight of a naked Fisher.

Finally they were both dressed. Fisher opened the door, letting in the now cooler and less heavy outside air. Fisher hurried out with the bag and their clothes and took them to the cabana before returning and jumping into the pool. Reynard followed, the cool water washing away the heat in a matter of seconds.

"There are people watching us," Reynard said once he came up and looked around. A group of girls about ten feet away were huddled together, giggling and watching the two of them.

"They probably think you're hot," Fisher said and then slipped under the water and glided away like a fish. Reynard followed with less grace. All his life he had been schooled on how to act in public. He had mastered entering a room and descending stairs properly by the age of seven. But he knew he would never be graceful in the water. His swimming was rough and sort of floppy. It always had been.

"Come on. The lazy river is over there, and we can just float in the shade." Fisher reached the stairs first. Reynard followed him out, and the girls giggled as they came out of the water. He turned toward the group, gave them a wink, and then turned away.

"You're terrible," Fisher told him as he handed him a float. "Those girls are going to remember you now."

They got into the flow of the water, and Reynard managed to get his bum in the center of the float, and then the water carried them downstream.

About halfway around, Fisher turned so his head was near Reynard's. He thought that Fisher might be going to kiss him. Instead Fisher said, "I don't want you to look, but there's a man watching us. I noticed him in line behind us on Storm Runner, and I saw him at the entrance to the cabanas. Now he's over by the bridge around there. Don't turn to look. But up ahead there's an exit and a channel across to the other side."

"Is he watching us?" Reynard asked.

"He's trying to be inconspicuous, but I think he's using his camera as a lookout of sorts." Fisher got closer.

Reynard grew nervous for the first time that day. Why couldn't he have a single day to himself—was it too much to ask? "What do we do?"

"Go into the cut-through," Fisher said as they approached. Reynard shifted over so the current would take him into the side channel. The plants and trees on the side cut off the view of the bridge. "Okay. Get off," Fisher instructed, and Reynard rolled off before standing in the stream.

"What about the float?"

"Just let it go," Fisher said and stepped back toward the main stream. "Come on." He led Reynard back to the nearest exit and out, then walked them briskly back to the cabana and into the relative invisibility of the area. "No one can get in unless they're supposed to."

"Okay. But now we have someone out there who seems to be following us, and we're stuck in here." He didn't want to hide out the rest of the day. Reynard had hoped that once the sun started to set they could ride some more coasters. Maybe that was too much to hope for. He had gotten some time to have fun, and maybe that was all he could expect.

"I'm going to go and see if I can find this guy. See if he's hanging around. Maybe the best tactic is to find out what he wants." Fisher pulled on a shirt, dried off his legs, and slipped into water shoes before leaving Reynard alone.

Shortly after Fisher left, one of the servers stopped by, and Reynard ordered mango smoothies. Then he did his best to settle back and relax. It didn't work. He kept thinking about the man watching them, what he wanted, and how his and Fisher's day had been ruined.

Fisher returned about the time their drinks came and slumped in the lounge. "I found him."

"And…?" Reynard took the drink, his belly clenching.

"He said he was just watching us and didn't want any trouble." Fisher took the smoothie and sipped it before continuing. "I honestly think he was completely shocked that I came up to him. He seemed a little shy and kind of scared."

"Okay. So he was what you would call a gawker?"

"Maybe. Once I spoke with him, some guys joined him. Unless your family is hiring geeky guys to try to find you, I think it was just my imagination."

Reynard hoped so. "Then let's finish these, change our clothes, and go on some more rides." He drank his smoothie and went to change. Fisher followed a few minutes later. They left their gear in the cabana, joined the flow of traffic through the back of the park to the racing coaster, and got in line.

"Prince Franz!" a female voice called just after he'd taken off his hat and glasses to stow them. He returned to the coaster train and got in his seat, purposely ignoring the call.

"I heard that," Fisher said once they were out of the station. "What do you want to do?"

"Nothing. Just ignore it and maybe they'll think they made a mistake." It wasn't like his family would hire teenage girls to try to follow him either. Still, the day's fun was quickly shifting into an exercise of evading people who might recognize him. They reached the top of the hill and raced down the other side, and Reynard tried to let go. But he was tense, and that sucked the fun out of the ride. By the time they reached the top of the second hill, he just wanted to get off.

"Scream it out," Fisher told him as they plunged downward once more. Reynard opened his mouth, yelling at the top of his lungs as the train dropped into a tight spiral, going faster as he yelled with everything he had. "Feeling better?"

"Yes," Reynard answered as they pulled to a stop outside the station.

"Good," he said quietly as they slid forward. Fisher lifted the lap bar, and Reynard got out and put on his hat and glasses before exiting the ride. He hurried down and out into the crowd of people with Fisher right behind him. Truthfully, he was trying to get lost in the others in the park.

"Do you want to go? We could get our things and…."

Fisher's phone chimed, and he pulled it out and paled. "It's from Gran." He tapped his phone and then turned it so Reynard could see. "It seems you've been identified and someone posted a picture of the two of us on Great Bear this morning. Others have been posted as well."

"Then we should go," Reynard said, letting Fisher lead him back to the cabana, where a security guard stood outside. "Damn," Reynard grumbled as he entered.

"Can we help you?" Fisher asked the guard.

"The manager of the park asked that we look after you while you're here, Your Highness," he answered, directing his attention to Reynard.

"Please tell him thank you, but that isn't necessary. Fisher here is more protection than I need, and the two of us will be leaving now anyway."

"I can walk you out," the guard offered.

"No. I don't want to draw any more attention." He was already pissed off that his family was going to zero in on the park. He and Fisher needed to get out of there fast before they swooped in, literally out of the air, to take him home. "But I appreciate the offer." Fisher had already gathered their things. Reynard put on his glasses and switched hats with Fisher before they left the area and strode through the park toward the exit.

"I think I get it now," Fisher said as they walked quickly without trying to draw too much attention.

"Since I was eight years old, I wanted to go to Disney, but I've never been able to. My father would never allow it, and even when my nanny offered to take us undercover, they refused." He continued walking, even when he thought he heard someone calling him. He wasn't sure, and the best thing to do now was to get back to the truck and get out of there. "The things most every kid gets to do, I couldn't." He stopped under the shade of a tree. "All I wanted was a chance to have fun like everyone else. I couldn't then, and it seems I can't now either."

They continued toward the exit, striding past the carousel and out of the park.

"Prince Franz!" someone called. He turned as a group of people raced toward him. Fisher took his hand, and they began to run through the parking area. More calls went up, and soon plenty of people had stopped to look. Fisher had the sense to slow down and join a group of people heading in their direction pushing strollers. When the next call went up, the others looked around, and Reynard did the same, staying near the group until they reached Fisher's truck and were safely inside and on their way out of the lot.

"It seems the picture has gone viral, especially within the park, since it was tagged. I bet everyone has been looking for you." Fisher turned onto the road leading away from the park. "I suspect it's only a matter of time before your family figures out where you are."

"Probably." He sighed and leaned back. All he had wanted was a little fun. Maybe it truly was too much to hope for.

Fisher pulled to a stop at a traffic signal. "Do you want me to take you to the house? You could pack your things, get in your rental, and head west. There are enough routes that it would be hard for them to track you, especially if you stayed away from the turnpikes and toll roads."

"Is that what you want me to do?" Reynard asked.

Fisher shook his head. "What I want doesn't really matter. One way or another, you'll be leaving and the last week or so will just be a memory." The sadness in his voice rang through as clear as a bell. "Your family isn't going to let you stay away forever. You have duties back home, and as much as I'd like to have you stay here with me, that isn't possible." He started forward when the light changed. "You need to decide what you want to do."

All Reynard could do was nod, knowing Fisher was right.

CHAPTER 10

"GRAN, WE'RE back," Fisher called.

"I'm in here," she answered, and Fisher went through to the living room, where his grandmother sat in her chair across from a stranger on the sofa. "This is Harvey. He was snooping around my backyard." She smiled, and Fisher noticed that he watched Gran like a hawk, his hands shaking a little. "I'm fine, but he's a little worse for wear."

"I was just trying to get a story, and she—" he sputtered.

"I saw him sneaking in and took him down. I may be old, but I can still defend myself if I have to." He was afraid she had overdone it and hoped Gran was truly okay.

"Then you brought him inside?" Fisher asked, wondering what Gran was thinking.

Gran looked at him like he was crazy. "I was trying to protect your friend. This sleaze was going to expose him. I thought it best to keep the police out of it. I figured he could sit here until you got back." She got into her stance and the reporter looked like he was about to wet himself.

Fisher sighed and turned to Harvey. "Did Gran use her self-defense on you?" She had taught classes in the eighties and nineties. This guy really picked the wrong person. When he'd first come out, Gran had shown him how to protect himself.

"The police might have something to say about her," Harvey snapped.

Fisher smiled. "I take it you're a reporter," he said, then waited until Harvey nodded. "And you had entered her property, and she thought you a danger. No police officer is going to take your side, especially since her grandson is a state trooper." He was really enjoying this. "Besides, can you imagine the story that would come out? You snuck into her yard in search of a story and got taken down by a woman in her seventies. I can see that going viral."

He expected the reporter to be embarrassed, but instead his jaw hardened. "And so will a story about Prince Franz hiding out in Central Pennsylvania. You can call the police, but I'll get out, and you won't be able to stop that story." He smiled. "Especially since he's right there." Harvey lifted his gaze. "I like the beard, Your Highness."

"Was it you who put the tracker on my car?" Reynard asked. Even after hearing him referred to as Prince Franz, he was still Reynard in Fisher's mind and probably always would be. "Why would you do that?" Reynard pressed without waiting for an answer. "Who do you work for? And why can't you just leave me alone?" Damn, when he peppered the guy with questions, the intensity was kind of hot.

"Do you think I'm going to tell you anything?" Harvey asked in return.

"Of course you are," Reynard said as he sat down. "You'll answer my questions, and then maybe I'll answer some of yours." Damn, the way he controlled the situation was impressive. "I think we have him over a barrel."

"How do you know?" Gran asked.

"Because he wants a story more than anything else, and he isn't going to want to leave until he gets it," Reynard answered levelly. "Now, will you answer my questions, or will you leave empty-handed and in handcuffs? I'm sure whoever you work for isn't going to be happy to get you out of jail, and these good people will deny that I was ever here. Your story will come off as a pack of lies with no proof, and in the end you'll have nothing." He seemed so sure of himself.

Harvey was practically salivating. "I saw you when you checked into the hotel. I was down there for dinner, and when you came in, I recognized you. I saw the car, and I put the tracker on it and figured I'd see where you went. I thought I might have a show when you stayed in town, and I tried to get close to you. But then I ended up in Virginia at a truck stop before figuring out I'd been decoyed. So I came back, and since the tracker showed you here for a while, I thought I'd take a look. The rental was in the garage, so… I took a shot."

"Who knows I'm here besides you?" Reynard asked.

"No one. You think I'm dumb enough to alert the troops and let them scoop my story?" He grinned.

"Are you sure talking to this guy is a good idea?" Fisher asked. He didn't trust Harvey, especially with the way he was looking at Reynard like he was a prize to be won.

"So why are you here?" Harvey asked.

"Not so fast," Fisher interjected. "I think there need to be some ground rules here." Even Gran leaned forward. "If Reynard answers your questions, you can't say anything about where he is." He crossed his arms over his chest, looking as intimidating as possible, and from the way Harvey swallowed, it seemed to be working. "Do you agree?"

Harvey nodded.

"You need to say it, and there are witnesses," Fisher said.

"I agree," Harvey replied. Fisher turned to Reynard and nodded slowly. He stood. Then the two of them wandered off through the house.

"Why are you here in Carlisle?" Harvey asked, and then the back door closed, cutting off their voices.

"You have to let him handle his own business," Gran told him. "But it's nice to see you so protective." She stood and patted his shoulder. "I'm going to get dinner started."

"What if that guy takes advantage of him?"

Gran paused at the entrance to the kitchen. "I'm sure he knows how to handle the press. He's probably done it much of his life." She held his gaze. "What is it you're really worried about?"

"Reynard is going to leave…." He took a deep breath.

"And you don't want him to," Gran supplied. Fisher nodded. "He has a life back home that he can't just turn his back on. You know that, and you have since he told you who he was." She tugged him into a hug. "What you did is fall in love with him."

"Gran, I like him and all—"

She smacked him on the shoulder. "Don't you go fibbing to me. I know what I see when you look at him. You get this smile, and he doesn't even have to be looking back. You know falling in love with someone is okay."

"Not when they're going to be leaving," he corrected.

She shook her head. "You can either lock away your heart and never feel anything or let yourself go and follow where it leads. You may get hurt, but you'll also know you're alive." She went into the kitchen, and Fisher figured he'd go outside to check out what was going on.

THE SCENE on the porch was surprising and made Fisher's blood heat. Reynard and Harvey sat in a pair of Gran's outdoor chairs, laughing together. That was the last thing he had expected. Harvey had that look again. Fisher didn't trust the guy. Something about him set off his police officer instincts, and yet he couldn't pinpoint what it was. Harvey truly seemed like he was basking in Reynard's presence, and maybe it was nothing, but Fisher's gut twisted and bells rang in the back of his head. But he'd been trained long ago to look for facts and to act professionally, and throwing the guy out because of a feeling would not endear him to Reynard.

"Fisher," Reynard said, and just like that, his expression changed. The laughter died away, but his gaze grew heated for a second. Damn, Fisher was getting used to the way Reynard looked at him. "We were just finishing up."

"One last question?" Harvey asked.

"All right," Reynard answered.

"What is your family going to think of your little vacation here among the common folk?" Harvey asked, glancing at Fisher, who stifled a groan at the dig. Fisher could see the angle he was trying to get at, and it set his teeth on edge.

Reynard seemed to take the question at face value, but Fisher wasn't sure that was all there was to it. "My parents are like any others and worry about me. I know that. But I just needed a little time to myself. I'd like to think they'd understand, but it's possible they'll be angry. Still, like every adult, I deserve a little independence.

That's what I came here for, and Fisher and his grand-mother have been kind enough to take me in."

"Did they know who you were?" The set of his lips made Fisher want to punch the guy. As if he and Gran had asked for anything from Reynard. This guy was a phony; Fisher would put money on it.

Reynard shook his head. "Not at first. I was just someone who needed their assistance, and they were good enough to lend a hand." He smiled at Fisher. "I would appreciate it if you didn't print their names. They don't need people camping outside their home trying to get to them. They are good people, as are the rest of the people that I've met here." Reynard was charming, and Harvey seemed completely taken in. "I think that's enough questions for now." Reynard leaned forward. "Remember our deal. I won't be speaking to any re-porters, so you get an exclusive story, but you have to wait a few days until I leave and keep Fisher and his grandmother out of it."

"I'll do my best," Harvey said.

Reynard leaned even closer and added an edge to his voice. "Listen to me. If you want more, then you need to play by the rules. It's that simple. Treat me right and I'll make sure that you get another interview in a few months, or maybe a heads-up on some interesting royal news. But all that dries up if you jump the gun."

Harvey was eating out of Reynard's hand, nodding like a bobblehead. "Okay." Fisher was pretty sure Rey-nard had just given the guy everything he wanted.

"Good." Reynard stood, and Harvey seemed to understand that it was time for him to go. Fisher won-dered if the guy was going to back away or something. At the very least he might have bowed slightly before leaving the yard.

"God," Fisher whispered. "You handled that like a pro." He still wondered if maybe Reynard was the one being handled, but he kept that to himself. No matter how he felt about Harvey, this was Reynard's game to play. Fisher would be there to back him up if he needed it.

"I am. I've been dealing with the press for some time, and if I wanted something from him, then I had to give a little. He's someone enamored with royalty, so I gave him a few minutes and answered his questions. None of them were very original, but I added a few nice tidbits for him, and he'll have a good story that will cause a sensation, especially locally."

"So you really think he'll do what you want?" Fisher asked.

Reynard nodded. "I gave him a good interview and extended a carrot that will be too good for him to pass up. I suspect he's hustling, trying to make a name for himself, and a couple stories from me could very well help get him on the map, and he knows it." He smiled. "Basically, he has more at stake if he breaks his word, and that should keep him honest."

"I suppose you're right." Though the thought of Reynard leaving sent a chill up his spine. But he knew their time together was limited, and now a definite time clock had been put on it. Reynard needed to be gone before the story about him being in town broke. Fisher knew that; he just wasn't looking forward to going back to being alone.

"HOW WAS your adventure in Hershey yesterday?" Clement Grant, one of the other troopers, teased as Fisher got ready for his patrol. Of course Fisher should have known that he would be in the pictures with Reynard and that some of the guys at work would recognize him. He had hoped to keep it quiet a little longer.

"I never pictured you as a royalty enthusiast," Fisher commented. He had always thought Clem much more interested in any sport with a ball: baseball, basketball, football… the guy could talk any of them for hours on end.

"I'm not. But Isabelle is, and she thought she saw you in one of the pictures. Did you happen to recognize him?" Clem asked. "Isabelle wants to know how it felt to sit next to a prince. Did you talk about anything or just ride the coaster?"

Fisher glanced over Clem's shoulder. "We rode the coaster. It was no big deal." If Clem wanted to think that they just happened to sit together on the ride, Fisher wasn't going to enlighten him. He checked the time and hurried out to his patrol car to get to work. He had a freeway to try to make safer and speeders to make slow down. Fisher had always wanted to be a police officer, but he hadn't figured on the solitary hours and the amount of time he'd spend sitting by the side of the highway watching traffic. He knew every new guy on the force took the shit jobs and worst shifts. He was lucky he had good work hours, even if the work wasn't all that exciting. Pushing thoughts of Reynard and their day at the park out of his mind, he headed out to start his day.

There must have been something in the water that morning, because he had to have written a dozen citations before noon. After the last one, Fisher returned to his vehicle, ready to sit a minute, when he received a message from Dispatch to return to the station.

Fisher acknowledged the message and pulled out of his parking spot, then took the next exit before driving to the station and parking in the lot. He wondered what was going on until he noticed a black sedan with darkened windows.

"Reporting as requested," he told Sandy, one of his fellow troopers.

"There's someone here to see you," she told him with wide eyes. She was a seasoned officer, and she'd seemed unflappable to Fisher, but something had certainly gotten to her.

"Thanks," Fisher said and went where she indicated. When he opened the door, he found a man in his early fifties, wearing a tailored suit, with intense eyes that seemed a little narrowed. "Can I help you?"

"Langley Bishop," he said. "I'm secretary to His Highness Prince Franz Reynard San Luis of Veronia, and if the pictures on the internet are accurate, then you have an idea where I can locate His Highness. We've had a number of people out looking for him for days with very little luck. And then pictures appeared online showing him with you." He stood tall, but he had a nervous energy about him.

"What do you think I can do? Yes, I was with the prince yesterday." He put on his best intense police officer expression—the one that said *don't mess with me*.

"We are trying to locate him," Langley said. "He's been gone almost a week, and we need to find him and bring him home. His family is becoming frantic." Small beads of sweat broke out on his forehead, and Fisher could just imagine the pressure he was under. "We can see to it that proper inducements are provided to those who can help."

Fisher narrowed his gaze. "Why should I or anyone tell you anything? If the prince isn't interested in being found, then that's his concern. Maybe the guy just needs a vacation from the likes of you. From what I know, the prince is an adult, and he's old enough to make his own decisions about what he wants and doesn't want."

"So you do know where he is?" Langley pressed.

Fisher didn't answer. He wasn't going to lie, but he didn't intend to give this guy anything without speaking to Reynard. The staring-down went on for a while longer until Langley blinked.

"Well…." Langley swallowed. "You see, there are other issues at the moment." Dark eyes seemed to flit around the room as though Langley were searching for any sort of help. It seemed to Fisher that he was growing desperate, and now he was curious why.

"I see," Fisher said. "What sort of issues?"

Langley cleared his throat. "I'm going to assume that you know where His Highness is and that you can get a message to him. You see, when His Highness took off, everyone thought it was a jaunt and that he'd return in a few days. Then it dragged on longer, and let's just say that while there was concern, we knew he was all right through one of his security detail. But in the past day… things have changed." Langley paused and seemed to think before his shoulders slumped slightly. "If you know where the prince is and can get a message to him, please tell him that the tiger cub is ill."

Fisher tilted his head slightly. "Is that some sort of code?"

"Please just give him the message," Langley said with what might have been genuine worry. "It's very important that he knows what's happening. The prince will know what he needs to do." Langley headed for the door, and Fisher watched him go, wondering what the hell was going on. He wasn't sure if he liked or trusted

Langley, but he did seem truly concerned for Reynard, and Fisher figured it wouldn't hurt to relay the message—but tonight, after he got home.

FISHER FOUND himself checking to make sure he wasn't being followed, though he supposed that if Langley could find him at work, he probably had figured out where Fisher lived. He was relieved when the black car wasn't waiting at the curb. He parked and went through the back gate. Gran was weeding one of her gardens.

"Where's Reynard?" he asked.

"Inside," Gran said, and he hurried in. He found Reynard in the living room with music on, dancing and swaying those hips to the salsa beat. Now that was a sight.

"Join me," Reynard said, taking Fisher by the hands, tugging him into the dance. "It's fun, yes?"

Fisher smiled, but Reynard must have seen that something was wrong. His hips stilled, and he turned down the music. "Tell me."

"Langley Bishop stopped by the station and spoke to me. Apparently your family is worried, and they were able to trace me from the pictures from yesterday. He asked if I knew where you were, and I didn't tell him. But I suspect he'll be able to figure out where I live."

"True. But even my family isn't going to harass an officer of the law, and they don't know I'm here." He turned up the music once again. "I have only a few more days before my parents demand my return, and I want to make the best of them. On Friday I will take the car and go back to New York and, as you say, face the music." He seemed resigned, but the idea made Fisher ache. He wrapped Reynard in his arms and held him tightly, the dance coming to an end as Reynard pressed against him.

"I don't want you to go, okay?" It was time for Fisher to put his cards on the table. He owed himself—and Reynard—that. "I know you can't stay and that you have responsibilities you can't walk away from, even if you wanted to take a vacation for a few days." He stopped speaking and put his mouth to better use, taking Reynard in a kiss that Fisher poured everything he had into. All the passion of their week together—the heart, the desperation at him leaving—it was all there, and Reynard returned every bit of it.

"I don't want to leave you either," Reynard whispered hoarsely when he pulled away. "I finally found someone who likes me for me, but I have to go. You know that. But we have a few more days."

Fisher was tempted to say nothing and take those few days. If he delivered the message Langley had asked him to, it would rob him of that time.

But he couldn't do it. "Langley gave me a message for you. He said to tell you the tiger cub is ill."

Reynard stilled, closing his eyes. He didn't move, and then he began to shake. Fisher held him tighter while Reynard quivered. Fisher didn't know what the message meant, but it had a powerful effect.

"The message… it means that my brother is seriously ill. I have to go home right away."

And just like that, Fisher's heart dropped to the floor.

CHAPTER 11

EACH MEMBER of Reynard's family had a code name. His father was *tiger*, his mother *tigress*, and he was *baby cub*. His brother had been designated *tiger cub* since before he was born. Fisher hated his code name and bristled every time it was brought up. But like so many things in his family, he had no say in the matter. Reynard was told the way things would be, either by his parents, the court, or the damned government; he was never asked. Hell, he was a grown man and would carry the code name *baby cub* until the day he fucking died.

"You got all that from, what, that little message?" Fisher asked, and Reynard briefly explained the code and what the message meant.

"I need to message Langley and then pack and get on the road to New York. He can arrange transportation home."

Fisher still held him, and Reynard wished he could stay in those arms forever. The surprising thing was that after only a week, he felt at home in them, like nothing could touch him, not even his family, as long as he was right here.

"Okay. Then go get your things. I'll make a few phone calls and talk to Gran." Fisher backed away and left the house, already speaking on the phone. Reynard went back to the guest room he had hardly even slept in and put his things in the hotel laundry bag. He also used his temporary phone to call Langley.

"I got your message."

"Thank goodness. Your family is—" Langley rushed the way he usually did.

"How is Albert? What's wrong with him?"

"The doctors aren't certain. Apparently he has been having breathing issues. The current theory is a kind of pneumonia. He is in stable condition at Queen Charlotte Hospital, and the last report was that he was resting. Your father wants you home as quickly as possible."

Of course he did. Make demands—that was how they worked.

"I'll—"

Reynard cut him off. "I'm going to be driving back to New York starting in the next hour. I'll arrive late this evening. Get me a hotel room and arrange the flight home. I'll leave first thing in the morning."

"I was instructed to—" Langley began.

"And I'm telling you what's going to happen." God, that felt so damned good. "Please make the arrangements."

"But your father," Langley said. "I can—"

Reynard cleared his throat. "I'll deal with him. You do what I'm asking you to. Get me a room at the Plaza for tonight, and I'll fly back in the morning." He would need a few hours to himself before he got on that plane and back on the carousel that was his life. Maybe the delay was just because he was being stubborn and was determined not to be told what to do. But everyone had been making demands on him all his life, and right now, his heart ached, and he needed a few hours to deal with that before he was forced to push it aside and put on the public face he knew would be required.

"Very well," Langley agreed, and Reynard thanked him and ended the call. Then he hefted the bag and carried it downstairs, where he found Fisher with a carry-all bag.

"I talked to the chief and explained the situation. I was granted a couple days' vacation. So I'll go with you to New York and make sure you get back to your family safely. I can take the train back, and one of the guys will pick me up at the station."

"You don't have to do that," Reynard said, even as relief washed over him. He would have one final night with Fisher before he left. It was less than he had hoped for, but it would give them a chance to say goodbye.

"We're wasting time," Fisher told him as Gran came in.

"You take care of yourself," she said, standing in front of Reynard, stroking his cheek. "Take charge of your life and live the one that you want. You felt the need to get away from who you were, so when you go back, be true to yourself and decide the course of your own future." She smiled, and then, when he leaned forward, she kissed his cheek. "Take good care of yourself, and you know you're welcome here any time, Reynard." She stepped back, and Fisher hugged his grandmother before leading the way out of the house and out to the garage. Fisher opened the overhead door and then slid behind the driver's seat of the rental car, and they headed back toward Reynard's life.

THE VALET at the hotel took care of the car with a promise to return the rental first thing in the morning. Reynard was met by the concierge as soon as he entered the hotel, and he and Fisher were escorted up to the suite Langley had arranged. As soon as they entered, Reynard found the man waiting for him. He looked skeptically at Fisher but said nothing before getting his notebook.

"Your flight will leave at eight local time. You are expected to arrive in Veronia in the afternoon tomorrow. You'll be expected at the hospital shortly after to visit your brother, and then your parents will meet with you at the palace."

"We've been on the road for hours," Reynard said flatly.

"I'll arrange for dinner to be brought up," Langley said.

"Very good. I'll see you in the morning," Reynard told him, then looked toward the door.

Langley nodded and did the little bow that signified he understood that he had been dismissed. But he cleared his throat instead of leaving.

"I understand there is more that you feel the need to review in what I'm sure will be great detail, but the return to my suffocating life will wait until the morning. It will have to." Langley turned, and Reynard sighed to himself. "Is there any further news on my brother?"

"He's sleeping and is still stable. The doctors are being cautious, but as of an hour ago, he was no worse."

"Thank you," Reynard said, and Langley left the room. The door closed with a *snick*.

"I love my brother. He's the best part of my family." He was relieved that Albert was holding his own. His brother was strong.

"Is there anything I can do?" Fisher asked.

"No, I don't think so." He sat on the sofa and leaned back, closing his eyes. "I'm sorry for all of this."

He felt Fisher sit down next to him. "Why? What are you apologizing for? Coming into my life and bringing a little light into it? Making me laugh this week? Giving Gran someone else to cook for and try to fatten up?" Fisher took his hand, entwining their fingers. "What is it that you're sorry for?"

"That it has to end," Reynard said softly. Fisher embraced him, and Reynard went into his arms so easily. Sometimes he had wondered if it was too much to ask for someone to simply care about him and not all the trappings of what he was. And the crappy thing was that once he had that, his life pulled him away from it before they really had a chance to get started.

A soft knock preceded Langley entering the suite with a cart of food. Reynard went quiet, not wanting Langley to overhear them talking. Not that he suspected Langley of being indiscreet, but if his parents asked about him and Fisher, Langley would feel obligated to answer.

"Thank you," Fisher said. "Have you eaten?"

"Yes. Thank you," Langley answered as he began setting up the food on the elegant table near the windows. Once he was done, he left the room, closing the doors behind him.

"Is he always like that?" Fisher asked. "I've known the guy, like, three minutes, and he seems as stuffy as they come." He extended his hand and tugged Reynard to his feet.

"Welcome to my world. Ritual and protocol rule the day. Langley has a certain air about him. It's his job to make sure that I'm properly dressed for every occasion. He also keeps my schedule so that I'm on time. He's the person I rely on most and who knows the most about me. And he was also hired by and works for my parents."

Fisher nodded. "So that's where his loyalties lie. He may help you, but he could go tattling to Mom and Dad about everything you do." They sat down, and Fisher waited, looking over to Reynard.

"Take what you want. There's plenty."

"I know, but…." Fisher shrugged. "You're changing by the minute. At Gran's, you were just Reynard, but now I can see the prince coming out. You aren't the same… and yet I know you are. What you allowed me to see at Gran's was the real man inside, and I know all this is just public trappings, but the way you just slipped back into it… I don't know." He took some of the chicken in white wine sauce and vegetables and tasted a tentative bite. Then he dug in the way he would at home. "This is really good."

"I'm glad you like it," Reynard said, eating more slowly. His instinct was to correct Fisher the way he would have been corrected if he had eaten as quickly as Reynard. At royal dinners, once the king finished a course, it was over and the plates were removed, so they were all trained from an early age to eat slowly, allowing the guests a chance to eat.

"I do," Fisher said, his gaze roving around the room. "This is sure a far cry from Gran's house." He sighed and rolled his eyes. "And here we put you up in the guest room." He half smiled.

Reynard placed his hand on Fisher's. "I was more comfortable in your guest room than I've ever felt anywhere." He lowered his gaze to the table. "Sometimes I feel like I'm just playing a part for everyone around me."

"Then don't," Fisher said. "Be yourself. Let some of the person that you've let me see come out. I know you can't just be Joe Guy-on-the-Street, because that's not you either, but you don't have to bury yourself under layers of what your family thinks they want. You be your own person."

"That's easy for you to say. You don't have my parents watching every move you make," Reynard countered forcefully.

Fisher set down his fork. "And you think I don't know what having others watch me is like? I was a scared, closeted gay kid in a public school in Central Pennsylvania. I thought everyone saw everything I did. I did my best to wear the kinds of clothes the other kids wore and cut my hair the way they did. I talked the way they did and went out with girls. I felt like a complete phony because that wasn't me. I was hiding, and it wasn't until Gran asked why I was so unhappy…." The softness that overtook Fisher's features was breathtaking.

"Let me guess, she told you to stop it," Reynard said with a smile before taking a small bite of the rich chicken dish.

"No. She asked me why I was so sad and lonely all the time. She sat me in her living room and said that she knew I was unhappy, but the only person who could make me happy was me. That if I didn't like things, then I had to change and be who I wanted to be… so I did. I told Gran that I liked boys, not girls, and that I hoped she didn't hate me. I remember Gran telling me not to be daft, and then she hugged me tight and said she loved me." A crack snuck into Fisher's voice for only a second, but it was there. Reynard was coming to love Fisher's strength, as well as the fact that he could be vulnerable. That vocal wobble touched Reynard's heart, and he paused with his knife hovering over his plate at how much leaving Fisher was going to hurt.

Suddenly he wasn't the least bit hungry. Still, he ate a few more bites because he felt he should and then set down his knife and fork, reached for his glass of wine, and drank down the entire glass.

"Hey," Fisher said as Reynard reached for the bottle. "Don't drink too much." Fisher placed his hand on top of Reynard's around the glass. "I know what's going to happen tonight and what all this means." He stood and came around to where Reynard sat. "We can talk about it… or you and I can make the most of what time we have left." Fisher leaned down and took Reynard's lips in a kiss that nearly toppled him and the chair with its force.

Thoughts of anything other than what Fisher was doing to him sailed out of his head. Reynard managed to set the glass back on the table and then wound his arms around Fisher's neck. Fisher pulled away, his gaze boring into Reynard's with so much heat, sweat broke out on his forehead.

Fisher tugged him to his feet. They left the table, and Fisher propelled him toward one of the bedrooms. Reynard didn't pay much attention to geography until they tumbled onto the soft bed. Fisher pressed him against the mattress, the kissing intensifying as if Fisher couldn't get enough.

Reynard found himself feeling the same way, giving as much as he took, needing to touch and taste, to impress those sensations deep into his memory. Reynard would never forget Fisher's hands—slightly rough yet gentle, expressive—and the way he slipped one under his shirt, splaying it against his belly without moving. Just holding it there, teasing Reynard with its heat. He squirmed, and Fisher kissed him deeper, tongue sliding between his lips, taking complete possession of his mouth. Reynard sighed and gave himself over to the pleasure. "Don't stop…."

Fisher pulled back. "Not going to. Now either get this shirt off or it's not going to survive." The grate in Fisher's voice had him undoing his shirt in seconds. Reynard squirmed out of it as Fisher tugged off his own, that powerful chest and cut belly making Reynard's mouth water. He wrapped his arms around Fisher's waist, burying his face against him, inhaling his rich, warm scent, tasting the salt of his skin. Fisher wound his fingers through Reynard's hair, lightly tugging him back and taking his lips once more.

Damn, Fisher had sexy ways of taking back control. He never spoke a word about it, but his strength and gentleness had Reynard wanting to let him have the power over their pleasure. "You look so damned good." Fisher sucked at the back of Reynard's neck, first one side and then the other, before pressing him back down.

He worked open Reynard's pants and then swore under his breath. "I need some things out of my kit." He backed away and stood beside the bed. "I'll be right back. Be naked when I return." He turned away, and Reynard immediately got his shoes, socks, and pants off and lay in the center of the bed. His cock ached, he was so hard, and Reynard stroked himself slowly to keep up the delicious anticipation.

"Fuck, that's beautiful," Fisher crooned when he returned. He set the kit next to the bed before shucking his shoes and popping the buttons on his tight jeans. Reynard drew closer, waiting for the fabric to part before sucking Fisher between his lips and tasting him hard and fast. There was no way he was going to get enough of him, not in a single night. Hell, he doubted there was enough time left in the universe for him to stop wanting Fisher. He pushed aside that they only had tonight and threw himself into giving Fisher

memories that would last forever. "Jesus," Fisher said
as he backed away. "It's going to be over before it gets
started if you keep that up."

That had been the entire point, but Fisher climbed
onto the bed, took Reynard's cheeks in his hands, and
kissed him, this time more gently but with even more
urgency, sending waves of excitement running through
Reynard. The waves built as Fisher covered him.

"I want you," Reynard said softly.

Fisher grinned, and then before Reynard knew what
was happening, Fisher rolled him facedown on the bed.
"Are you ready for me?" Fisher spread Reynard's legs
and buried his face between them. Reynard gasped as
Fisher did things to him he had only dreamed of or seen
in movies he watched only when his internet couldn't be
monitored. He gasped as Fisher drove his tongue deep
and wet, hot breath floating over sensitive skin.

"Oh God," Reynard cried before lapsing into a
steady stream of French. He couldn't help it—the passion was too overwhelming, more than he had ever expected. Grabbing a pillow, he bunched his fists in the
plush down. He needed…. He wanted…. And the worst
thing was, he couldn't figure out anything beyond those
nebulous, fractured thoughts. All he knew was that he
wanted more, and Fisher delivered.

Fisher covered him with his body, and Reynard
barely heard the rip of foil through the haze of passion
that enveloped him. When Fisher sank into him, Reynard pressed back, taking him swift and deep, gripping
Fisher with his body the same way Fisher held Reynard
with his strong arms.

"I don't want to let you go," Fisher whispered
as he pulled back and then slid forward, their bodies
joining as Reynard's spirit melded with Fisher's. They

undulated together, not wanting to be apart, Sweat broke out over them as they filled the room with the sound and scent of their lovemaking.

"More… don't stop…," Reynard whimpered, his throat dry and maybe a little sore, but he didn't dare even think about it. If his mind wandered for a moment, he might miss something, and he couldn't bear that.

"Not going to," Fisher answered, driving them higher until he pressed to Reynard and held him tightly, and they reached the pinnacle together in an explosion of passion that left them both wrung out and panting before they collapsed onto the bedding. The only thing that Reynard could concentrate on, besides his need for air, was the fact that Fisher held him tightly. That was all that mattered.

"GET OUT," Fisher said firmly, tightening his arms around Reynard. Reynard cracked his eyes open just in time to see the bedroom door close. "Langley," Fisher explained to Reynard more softly. "I think he came in to get you up and got more of an eyeful than he was expecting." There was a hint of amusement in his voice. "I doubt he'll be doing that again."

Reynard chuckled. "I forgot to leave instructions with him, and he probably slipped into the usual routine." He checked the time and groaned before turning back. "I'm afraid it's time." He had to get up and out of bed. He had a long day of travel ahead of him.

"But it's four in the morning." Fisher rubbed his eyes as Reynard turned on one of the small bedside lamps.

"I know, but Veronia is six hours ahead, and the flight is about that long. I'll have to rest on the plane.

Hopefully I'll be able to, because when I hit the ground, it will be late afternoon and I'll have an entire day's work to finish."

Fisher sat up, the covers pooling around his waist. "Then why did you wait? You could have left last night."

Reynard leaned closer. "Then we wouldn't have had our time together."

"But you instructed Langley to make the arrangements for this morning before I said I'd come. How did you know?"

"I didn't. But I hoped," Reynard confessed. "I couldn't ask you to come here with me. But then again, I didn't think I'd have to." Reynard leaned against Fisher, who held him. "I know you, Fisher. You're the best man I've met, and you don't disappoint. You are the kind of man who would see me back to New York just because that way you'd know I was safe." Reynard kissed him. "But as much as I'd like, you can't see me any further. You have your life and your grandmother, and I have my family. We can't turn our backs on them."

"No. Gran needs me, and she's done so much for me. Besides, what would I do in Veronia? I'm just a police officer in a small town. You're a prince." Fisher shifted and slipped out of the bed. "I'll miss you, and for the record, I know you too. You're kind and thoughtful and more of a regular guy than you'd like to think. You put others before yourself. I know you felt the need to try to run away from your life for a while, but remember to just be the man I had the chance to get to know." Fisher kissed him once more. Then he dressed in the low light and left the bedroom.

Langley entered a few minutes later and began setting out Reynard's clothes. "We have to be at the airport in no later than half an hour. A helicopter will meet us on the roof in fifteen minutes. I have a detailed itinerary for when you arrive in Veronia."

"Of course you do," Reynard said when he finished dressing. "Thank you. We can review it on the plane." Reynard found Fisher seated at the table with a cup of coffee. He handed one to Reynard and let him take a few sips.

"I know you have to go." Fisher hugged him, and then they shared a kiss. Finally, Fisher got his bag, and Reynard's gaze followed him to the door. He didn't look away until it closed behind him. There was no going back now. His days of relative freedom were over, and he could feel the weight of duty settle on his shoulders.

"SIR, CAN we go over your schedule?" Langley asked.

Reynard looked away from the window, where the coast of Cornwall was just coming into view. Another hour and they would be preparing for landing. "Of course," he said softly, pulling his mind away from the thoughts of Fisher that he'd been buried in ever since takeoff. Langley had been good enough to leave him to himself, and Reynard was grateful, though now he needed something to occupy him or he was going to drive himself crazy. He had been tempted to instruct the pilot to go back more times than he could count. "Let me get my bag so I can take something for a headache and I'll be ready."

Langley brought his bag to him, and Reynard pulled out his travel pill case and took a Panadol before putting the bottle back. When he did, he noticed an envelope along the side of the bag. He motioned

for Langley to sit and pulled it out, then set the bag on
the floor next to his seat. He opened the envelope and
found a sheet of lined writing paper.

R—

*I know you have to go, and there are things I want
to tell you, but I don't think I can find the words in
person. Hopefully you'll read this after you've gone. I
want you to know that you and I had an amazing week
together, one that will live in my heart and memory
forever.*

*Time will dull the feelings we shared, as it does
everything, but know that what I feel for you was and is
real. We come from different backgrounds, but we came
together as equals, seeing each other for who we are…
not the trappings and circumstances that surround us.*

*Remember to be the amazing man you are no mat-
ter what. That's the person I fell in love with and the
one who will live on with me. You tried to run away
from your life, and because of that, I got to know the
real you. Let that man guide you and don't bury him
away. He's too precious and caring for that. Don't let
your family or anyone try to change him, and know that
you are loved for yourself… no matter what.*

Fisher

Reynard folded the letter and placed it carefully
back in the envelope, then slid it back into his bag.
"Can we go over my schedule in ten minutes?" He got
up without waiting for an answer and slipped into the
lushly appointed restroom in the family's private jet,
needing a few minutes to pull himself together.

CHAPTER 12

FISHER CLICKED off Harvey's story about Reynard and unclenched his teeth. He had been nervous about what the slimeball would write. He didn't trust the man, and everything Fisher read about him, including some of this other work, told him that he was right. The guy specialized in hatchet jobs, but the story about his prince had been honest and surprisingly kind. Maybe the lure of future stories really had been too good for him to pass up. Fisher's break was nearly over, and he wadded up the Kind bar wrapper and tossed it into the trash.

A knock on his passenger-side window drew his attention, and he lowered it.

"What's going on out here?" Wyatt asked, and Fisher unlocked the doors. Wyatt slipped into the passenger seat and closed the door. "You've been surprisingly quiet. Usually you're chatty, especially when parked by the side of the road with nothing but cars to watch."

"I've just been thinking a lot," he answered as a car zoomed by. Fisher clocked him at eighty before the guy saw him and put on his brakes. Fisher activated his lights and pulled out into traffic, adding his siren as he got up behind the speeder and pulled him over. Wyatt was already running the plates.

"The car was reported stolen," Wyatt said.

Just as Fisher called for backup, the car peeled out, and Fisher gave pursuit, with Wyatt providing a chatter of directional information to Dispatch. The vehicle didn't get far and was stopped a few exits ahead, and the suspect was apprehended and taken back to the station by one of the other units. Fisher would need to provide information and evidence about the initial stop, but the rest would be handled by one of the other troopers, and he returned to his initial traffic stop position.

"Well, that was exciting for, like, fifteen minutes," Fisher deadpanned.

Wyatt scoffed. "Shit, kid, that's the job. Hours of tedium and watching for a few minutes of activity. That's how it is, at least to start with. You know that."

"Yeah, I know, and I'm not really complaining. I like my job. I guess I didn't expect…." He wasn't sure what he wanted to say and let his thought trail off.

Wyatt clucked his tongue with a tiny smile. "Maybe this has nothing to do with the job and everything to do with a certain guy who went home earlier this week. Or should I say a certain prince who came to town." He snickered. "I saw the article."

"I bet half the station did," he grumbled. Sometimes the guys gossiped like hens. Most state troopers rarely came into the station. They spent their days on patrol in their areas. But that didn't mean they didn't talk to each other, and gossip could spread fast, especially if it was juicy.

"Why? It's not like cops are particular royalty watchers, and you were never mentioned in the article. The guys are none the wiser, though Quinton is going to be a little upset that he didn't get to meet him. I'm afraid you're going to have to explain to him why you didn't introduce the prince to your friends."

Fisher groaned, and Wyatt grinned. "You're teasing."

"Of course I am. Though Quint is jealous. Apparently he's a real royal follower. That's something I had no idea about until he saw the article and I explained that we'd stopped him for speeding. You should have heard all the questions he asked. I'm surprised he didn't inquire if he wore a crown while he was driving."

Fisher snorted and put his hand over his mouth. "Reynard isn't in line for the throne, so he won't wear a crown. He left quickly because his older brother was ill, but apparently Crown Prince Albert is making a slow but steady recovery." As much as he hated to admit it, Fisher searched the internet each morning for stories about Reynard and his family. He realized it could become an obsession, and he knew he needed to stop. It wasn't doing him any good.

"Look, I'm sensing that something happened between the two of you. I know you offered him a place to stay, and I'm thinking that maybe he didn't stay in the guest room?" At least Wyatt didn't seem like he was teasing. "Holy crap… you fell for the guy." The shock was almost comical. "How could you do that? He's a prince. You knew he was going to have to go home."

Fisher gripped the wheel as he watched the radar speed indicator of passing cars. At least it gave him something to look at other than Wyatt. "Like you had a choice when you fell for Quinton," he countered.

"Yeah, but Quint is a regular guy who got into some trouble. He wasn't a fucking prince." The way he said it, Reynard could have been from outer space.

Fisher's knuckles turned white. "What do you think Reynard is? He's a guy like anyone else. He made mistakes, and yeah, he had to go home. He has duties that he felt he couldn't walk away from. And he only

wanted some time away from all that. He's entitled to
that. Reynard still puts his pants on one leg at a time,
just like the rest of us."

Wyatt grew quiet and then nodded. "What are you
going to do?"

Fisher shrugged. "There isn't a damned thing I can
do. The two of us had an amazing week, and I let my
heart get involved. Not that I could have stopped it. So
now I'll wait to let it heal and then move on. It isn't
like I can fly to Europe and go knocking on the palace
door. 'Hi, I'm Fisher Bronson, can Reynard come out
and play?'" He knew there wasn't a snowball's chance
in hell that he would be able to get anywhere near the
place, even if he was dumb enough to jump on a plane.
No, he had to give himself a chance to get over it and
move on.

Wyatt patted his shoulder and then opened the door
and got out. "If you need anything, you can call any
time. You know that." He waited until Fisher thanked
him before closing the door and returning to his patrol
vehicle. Wyatt pulled out around him, leaving Fisher
with his thoughts and the speed of traffic.

"THAT MAN was hanging around the house today,"
Gran said as soon as he came in the back door. Fisher
was sweaty and tired. "You look like hell," she added
for good measure.

"Thanks." He hummed. "Which man?" he added
when his tired mind caught up.

"That reporter that you didn't like. I was in the
backyard, and he was peeking over the fence. When
I saw him, I went over to the gate and asked what he
wanted. He said he was just looking at my garden. I

think he was trying to see if Reynard was still here. I told him to go away or I'd call the police and report him as a Peeping Tom. Then he left."

"Good, Gran." He smiled at her and would have hugged her, but his clothes were sticking to him. The air-conditioning in his car had gone out an hour before the end of his shift. "I'm going to go inside and get cleaned up. Then I thought we could go out for dinner."

"Where?" Gran asked. She was picky about her food.

"Anywhere you want. So figure out where to go and we'll head out in half an hour." He went inside and right up to his room. He kicked off his shoes, and one slid under the bed. He bent to pick it up and saw a hint of yellow fabric. When he reached for it, his fingers touched silk. It was one of Reynard's shirts. Fisher remembered it, or more importantly, how Reynard had looked out of it once Fisher had stripped it off him. It must have gotten pushed under the bed.

He brought it to his nose, inhaling Reynard's scent from the fabric. He closed his eyes and sighed. Then he folded the shirt and set it on top of his dresser. Damn, he missed the man like an ache, and he had no idea what to do to make it go away.

Fisher showered and dressed, then joined Gran downstairs. "Where did you want to go?"

"Hamilton. We can get Hot-Chee dogs." She loved those, and Fisher wasn't in the mood to tell her no. "They only take cash."

"I know. I have enough," Fisher told her. "Let's go eat." They headed out to the truck, and he took off downtown and was lucky enough to find a place to park right in front. He and Gran went inside, and they took the only empty table in the place. Gran excused herself and went back to the restroom while Fisher looked over the menu.

"Hello," a familiar voice said.

Fisher lowered the menu. "What do you want?" he asked Harvey, who sat in Gran's space.

"I was looking for your friend."

Fisher shrugged. "Don't you follow the news you actually cover? He returned to Europe days ago. His brother was ill, as you're probably aware, and he had to go back there."

Harvey leaned over the table. "So were you and the prince lovers? Did he jilt you and run back home? My paper will pay plenty of money for a good story. My last piece was good, but I need more juicy information, and I can pay for it." The look in his eyes made Fisher feel dirty, and all he wanted was to get this man away from him.

"My grandmother is having dinner with me, and you're in her seat. Get up and leave us alone. I can call the owner and have you removed." He kept his voice level.

"Just one more question—how much will it take to get something juicy?" Harvey asked, leaning forward as though Fisher had encouraged him.

"Get out," Fisher said before turning around. He motioned to the owner behind the counter up front, and he came over. "This man is leaving. Can you please show him out? And make sure he pays his bill and tips his server generously. She probably had to put up with a lot."

"Of course, Fisher," Ron said.

Harvey got up. For a second he looked like he was going to try for some clever parting shot, but in the end he was escorted out, and Gran sat down in her seat.

"Was that that awful reporter?" she asked with a sneer.

"It was. Ron was good enough to show him the door," Fisher told her. "You might want to wipe off the seat in case he left some slime on it."

Gran chuckled as she picked up her menu.

They had their usual discussion about what they wanted to eat, and once Gran had her cup of coffee, she leaned forward. "You've been out of sorts since Reynard left. Are you really okay?" She sipped from her mug, looking at him like she did when she knew he'd been sneaking cookies.

"I am."

She shook her head. "No, you're not. You mope around the house and schlump off to work. You always loved your job, but now you just go through the motions. I've seen it, and I suspect your friend Wyatt has too."

Fisher shrugged. "What am I supposed to do?"

Gran rolled her eyes like he was being dumb. "You need to call him."

"How? Call the palace and ask for the Department of Princes?" He smirked, and Gran lightly smacked his hand.

"Don't get sassy with me," she chastised. "I changed your diapers. I can certainly spank you if you need it." She sighed, set her mug down, and opened her purse to pull out a sheet of paper that she slid over to him.

"What's this?"

"His phone number. This one is his personal cell in Veronia."

Fisher stared at the handwritten numbers on the paper. "But why did he give it to you?"

"He said that if I needed anything, I was to contact him. Reynard told me that I was a wonderful hostess and that I helped make his visit special. He said that if we needed anything, to call." She reached across the table. "I'm not sure exactly what he meant, but I'd say you need something pretty badly—him." She patted his hand and then pulled hers away as Sophia came to the table to take their order.

She and Gran talked for a few minutes. Gran was a regular, so she knew just about everyone who worked at the restaurant. Fisher continued staring at the paper, wondering what he was going to do.

"Those numbers aren't going to jump off the page and bite you in the nose. Put them in your phone and then give me the paper back." Fisher did as she asked. "You can't call now anyway. It's too late. You'll have to wait until the morning. Now let's have a nice dinner and you can tell me about your day."

FISHER BARELY ate or paid attention to anything the rest of the evening, and he slept like shit because he was constantly checking the time. Finally, after waking again at four in the morning, he checked his phone and pressed Send. He almost hung up, but then the line buzzed and he closed his eyes in the dark room.

"Bonjour."

Fisher would know that voice anywhere, and his heart skipped a beat. "Reynard, it's me, Fisher," he said, throat clenching. "It's good to hear your voice." He wasn't sure what they would talk about and wished he had put more thought into possible subjects of conversation.

"It's good to hear from you too," he said softly. "Give me just a moment." Fisher waited, staring up at the ceiling in the darkness. Then Reynard came back on the line. "I'm so glad you called."

"How is your brother?"

"Much better. Albert is recovering and should start light duties in the next few days. The king and queen are very relieved." He suddenly sounded very formal. "Langley has just joined me."

"I see. Am I bothering you? Is there a better time for me to call to talk to you, or…?" Maybe this was foolish and he was just being needy. Reynard had many things he needed to do, and talking to Fisher was probably just wasting his time.

"You never bother me. I have a meeting with the king in half an hour. I thought I would take a page from your book and try to do something of my own. Gran got me thinking while I was there. We have a number of royal parks and open areas. I want to turn one of them into a botanical park with sculpted gardens and specimen plants and make it open for everyone." He sounded so excited. "But I need his permission, and change is something he never takes well. If Albert proposed it, he'd probably agree, but since I'm the one with the idea, he's likely to say no out of habit." Reynard sighed. "Anyway, you didn't call to talk about that. Is there something you needed?"

"Just to hear your voice," Fisher answered before he had a chance to think about it. Closing his eyes, he could almost feel Reynard in the room with him. "Before you say anything, I know I'm being stupid. I have Gran and my job here, and you have your duty in Veronia. Maybe even calling was a bad idea, because it only makes me want to see and touch you even more, but I couldn't help it. As soon as Gran gave me the number, I just had to use it." The line grew quiet once he was through, and the silence stretched on. Fisher became nervous and wondered if he had completely scared Reynard off.

"I know exactly how you feel," Reynard said finally. "I had my finger on the button to call you at least a dozen times, but I didn't know what could possibly come of it. And now that you called, I feel like a total wanking idiot."

"You aren't, and you know it."

"I have to get ready to meet with the king, but I'll call you in the next few days. I promise. We can talk some more." Reynard's voice seemed a little lighter than it had when he first answered the phone. "And get some sleep. I know it's the middle of the night there." Reynard's voice lowered and became thicker. "I'd ask you some particular questions since my imagination is going a little wild right now. But I can't." He chuckled softly.

"We'll talk soon," Fisher said, and then Reynard was gone. He set his phone by the side of the bed and rolled over, trying to relax and put Reynard out of his head, but it seemed the call had only set his mind to spinning even more.

"ARE YOU still at work?" Reynard asked when he called two days later just as Fisher was getting home.

"I'm in the truck, pulling up to the house." He groaned as a familiar figure headed up the sidewalk toward where he'd parked. "Harvey is headed my way. The sleaze has been making a real pest of himself. He actually asked me questions when Gran and I were out having dinner." He brought the phone to his ear, turned off the engine, and opened the door, transferring the call back to his phone. He was still wearing his uniform, and that seemed to give Harvey pause. Fisher used the time to go into the house without acknowledging the guy was there. "I'm inside now."

"I'm sorry he's being a pest. I never meant for that to happen. I actually thought he would be satisfied, especially with the carrot I left him. But obviously not." He sounded disappointed. "My father would have told me not to speak to the man at all. Ignore him and make no comment. Let the palace speak for us and say nothing else. That's what Dad has always done, and I thought him old-fashioned, so I did what I wanted to do, and now I'm over here and you have to deal with this reporter alone."

"I can handle it. If Gran finds him hanging around again, I think she'll take a rake to him. I know how to take care of people like him, and he isn't going to get a story or anything from us. I think he's probably just chasing his tail because you're gone and the only connection left is me." He smiled to himself. "Let's talk about something else. This guy isn't worth worrying about… not now." His throat ached.

"Then what do you want to talk about?" Reynard asked.

Fisher waved to Gran and went up to his room and closed the door. "Oh, I don't know. What are you wearing?" he asked, grinning at the groan from Reynard.

"Nothing the slightest bit sexy. Trousers, a shirt, and old shoes that have seen better days but are too comfortable to pitch in the bin. This afternoon I was out for a ride on a four-wheeler checking out a section of the grounds for one of Albert's projects. I really think I found something I'm good at—gardening—thanks to you and your Gran."

The heat that had begun to build slipped away, but Fisher smiled anyway. "I'm glad. You really seemed at loose ends when you were here." He was happy for Reynard, truly—and pleased that they'd had something to do with his newfound purpose. "How did things go with the king?"

"About as I expected. He was skeptical, but he didn't shut the door completely and asked me to put together some plans and ideas for what I want to do."

Fisher wanted to jump up and down. "Dude," he said. "That's great."

"Excuse me?"

"The king is interested. I don't know him, but if I were to come up with an idea to my captain and he thought it intriguing, he'd ask me to put together more details. That's what your dad did. Show him you're serious. Get some local experts involved. Tell them what you want to do and get their help. Show them the dynamic, amazing guy you are and they'll want to get involved and help you."

"You really think so?" Reynard asked.

Fisher smiled. "I think you should put together a detailed plan with a drawing and layout of what you want to do and where. Give him something he can see, and then I think the king will give his permission. Think of it this way. If he'd just said yes…." Fisher paused because he didn't want to hurt Reynard's feelings or say the wrong thing. If they were face-to-face, he could see him and read his expression, but over the phone, this was harder. "That would be too easy. Show him you have a solid idea and plans to bring it about."

"Yes," Reynard said. "I can see that. Okay. And I know just the people to contact." The excitement in Reynard's voice made Fisher smile.

"I'd love to see the plans, and hope that when the garden is done, I'll be able to visit it someday." He'd only reminded himself just how far away Reynard was.

"You'll get a royal invitation. I promise," Reynard said as muffled voices sounded behind him. "Not now," Reynard said with a slight snap in his voice. "I need to go. Apparently my presence is being requested. It seems my father can't sleep, and he's asking to see me." It had to be nearly midnight there.

"Go do what you have to and then get some rest." He wanted to say that he wished he could be there in bed next to him. "I need some myself."

"Why?" Reynard asked. "Are you not resting?"

Fisher paused and then decided to go for the truth. "Not really. I got used to having a certain man with cold feet in bed next to me, and I haven't been able to get him out of my mind or, it seems, sleep well without him." He cringed at how needy that sounded and wished he had kept his mouth shut. All this wishing and wanting wasn't going to change anything, and he needed to try to let it go. These calls weren't helping, but damn it all if Fisher didn't look forward to them, and once he hung up, he always waited for Reynard to call again or for a time when he could. What he really wondered was how in the hell he had let Reynard get so deep under his skin and what the fuck was he going to do about it.

"I know how you feel," Reynard said quietly, and then the call disconnected.

Fisher swallowed and tossed the phone on his bed. He wiped his eyes and then got busy, changing out of his uniform and into comfortable clothes. Only then, once he had had a chance to pull himself together, did he leave the room to see what Gran was up to.

"YOU NEED to call your friends and get your butt out of this house," Gran scolded the following week. "You go to work, and when you get home, you carry that phone around like you're a drowning man and it's a life

preserver." She set her trowel in her garden cart and
got to her feet. "Get out of this house. You're driving
me crazy. I'm having dinner with some of the ladies
from the garden club. We're doing some planning for
the year."

"I'll just make some dinner and…." He didn't feel
like going out.

"Fine." She shook her head. "But sitting here alone
isn't going to help." She walked slowly across the grass.
"I know you miss him and it isn't getting much better.
Let your friends help you. Call a few of them and get up
a game of poker while I'm out. Just don't smoke in my
house. I've got chips and snacks in the pantry for you."
He should have known that Gran would have paved the
way. "Wyatt and his partner are nice boys, so give them
a call." She would probably make the call for him if
Fisher didn't agree. "And don't forget Casey and Bertie. The kids can all play in the backyard. They aren't
going to hurt anything while you boys sit around and
have a beer." She patted him on the shoulder. Fisher
stood still, just listening to the breeze.

"Those boys aren't going to call themselves. I can
do it for you," Gran said.

Fisher laughed. "Didn't you already do that?" he
called after her.

She turned around. "Of course I did. They'll all
be here in an hour, so shave and get cleaned up and
dressed. But it would be nice if you called to firm up
plans and then explain away why your nosey grandmother is making play dates for you at your age." She
went inside, and Fisher called Wyatt and Casey, who
had indeed received a call from Gran. And they were
happy to come over. As he talked, he checked the refrig-
erator and found hot dogs, burgers, and all the fixings

ready to go. Sometimes Gran was just too much, but she cared—Fisher never doubted that. There was even lemonade for the kids. Gran thought of everything.

CASEY TOOK charge of the grill, because that was what he usually did when they got together. His and Bertie's kids were running through the yard, playing with Jackson's toddler son, as happy and content as any child Fisher had ever seen. Those children had been through a lot, with their mother leaving them alone and disappearing. But Casey and Bertie had done wonders with them. They seemed happy, energetic, and as loud and day-brightening as kids should be. They had developed a game of hide-and-seek and were off as Fisher brought the last fixings out of the house.

"What has your gran so concerned that she called us?" Bertie asked. "Not that we're complaining. You've been scarce the past few weeks." He spread things out and got places for the kids all set up and ready.

"Fisher is in love, and he's had his heart bruised," Wyatt teased.

"That's not very nice," Jackson chastised lightly. "I take it the prince turned out to be a frog."

Fisher shook his head. "The prince turned out to be a prince, just not *my* prince, as it happens. He's back in Veronia. He and I talk every couple of days, and I really liked him."

"He fell in lurve," Wyatt interjected, and Jackson rolled his eyes. "And now he can't figure out how to wash that man out of his hair."

"How Rodgers and Hammerstein of you," Bertie said with a smile. "But seriously. What do you want to do?"

Fisher sat down and grabbed a beer from the cooler Wyatt had brought. "I don't know. If he was just a guy, I'd probably make plans to go over to visit him when I got some time off. I've only used a day of my vacation, not that I have all that much of it."

"You get two weeks, and you've been with us a year already," Chase said as he joined them at the table. "And if I'm not mistaken, he came to Carlisle to get away from all the royal stuff. So maybe your prince is more of a normal guy than you expect."

Fisher nodded and drank half the bottle of beer just to numb his heart a little. "And maybe I just need to walk away before I get hurt even more. He's on the other side of the Atlantic, and I'm here. I'm beginning to think I should simply go on and try to forget about him."

Casey and Wyatt nodded, but Jackson frowned at them. "And do you know what Reynard wants? Have you even talked to him about what's possible, or are the two of you too 'manly' to actually talk about what you really want and just keep circling each other like boxers in a ring? I mean, he may be waiting for you to offer to come for a visit, but isn't sure what you want."

"I don't know about all of you, but I thought we were going to drink beer and have some fun, not be Dear Abby," Bertie said as he brought over a plate of cooked hot dogs and burgers. "But if you want my opinion, talk to him and then arrange to go over there and see him. That way you can either say goodbye and walk away or figure out if your prince is really a frog in disguise or if he's Prince Charming. And you aren't going to find out until you see him again—and this time on his turf. What if whatever is between you has cooled? At least you get a vacation, and you can come home and go on with your life. Then you'll know." He set down the plates and called the kids to the table.

They trundled over, and Jackson helped Callum while Bertie and Casey got the others settled before they all fixed their plates. Fisher wished he knew what to do. Part of him wanted to hop on a plane and see Reynard once again. It seemed like such a leap of faith... too much. Yet he was the one who told Reynard to go for it when it came to what he wanted from his father. Maybe he needed to take his own advice.

CHAPTER 13

REYNARD'S SHOES snapped on the highly polished marble floors as he went to answer his brother's request. He reached the impressive stairs and ascended. Plush carpets ran through the hallways of the bedroom level of the palace, muffling his footsteps as he passed antiques of various periods collected by generations of his family. Not that he had ever particularly noticed them, at least not until he returned from Gran's home in Carlisle. Now he tended to notice a great deal more of the luxury that surrounded him. Reynard reached Albert's door, knocked, and entered the sitting room.

Albert sat on a lounge with his feet up. He was dressed lightly and had a blanket over his legs. "What can I do for you?" Reynard asked. He was really coming to resent how everyone in the family—including his brother—called for him like he was at their beck and call. "I came as soon as you summoned me."

Albert sat up. "What's wrong with you? And what's with the attitude all the time?" He pulled the blanket a little higher in the cool room.

"I have things I'm working on, but you called me like I'm some dog who's supposed to fetch your slippers." He glared at his brother. "The king and queen do the same thing. Why do you think I went off on my own?" He crossed his arms. "Being on my own was much more preferable to being the spare in a system where I have no place other than as the lackey for all of you." He held Albert's gaze, determined to stick it out.

Ever since they were kids, Albert had been the one in charge, the dynamic older brother who knew and understood his place in the world. Albert was confident and at peace with his lot in life. He would eventually be king; it was that simple. "What is it you want?"

"I asked Phillipe to find out where you were and say that I'd like you to come see me." Albert lowered his gaze. "I wanted to speak with you, not get into an altercation, though I think this casts some light on what I wanted to speak about." He pulled the blanket away and stood, then walked gingerly over to the sofa, where he sat once more. "Please sit down."

Reynard took the chair across from his brother. "What is it? I have a meeting in half an hour."

"About this garden project of yours?" he asked.

"Yes. I'm meeting with glasshouse architects and landscapers and gardeners. We're formulating detailed plans of what we'd like to accomplish. I don't want this to be some huge formal royal garden, but something special that the people can enjoy. I want this to be for them. The area I'm proposing isn't used for anything. It was cleared some time ago, and now the area is overgrown and kind of scrubby. Our grandfather intended to use the area for something, but his plans can't be located. Why?"

"I like the idea." Albert leaned forward. "And I've contacted the royal staff to—"

Reynard put his hand up. "Excuse me. This is my project, and I want to do it."

Albert glared. "I was only trying to help." He sat back.

"Maybe this is something I'd like to do on my own and in my own way," Reynard countered. "I don't want the royal gardeners. This isn't going to be something out of the eighteenth century that I'm trying to recreate. I want this to be modern and fresh—clean and colorful, rather than linear and fussy, with a show greenhouse that people can walk through, and even a space where weddings or parties can be held."

"But royal events—"

"Open it to the people. This is for them." Reynard felt his excitement growing. "I want to sponsor this for the people, not for us. This isn't about us. That's what I'm trying to get across to everyone. Father is always saying that we have to think of the people we serve, and that's what I'm trying to do here." He hoped he could make Albert understand.

Albert sat still for a few seconds and then nodded. "I think your idea is even better than what I thought." He smiled, and Reynard relaxed slightly. "You do things the way you think best, but know that the royal gardeners and landscapers will be available to support you. They're curious too, about what you have in mind." He sighed and seemed tired. "I was honestly trying to help, and you've been short-fused and cross since you returned. What is happening with you? Everyone has noticed it."

"I'm sure I'm the topic of disappointing dinner conversations all over the country," he retorted sarcastically.

"See, that's just it. You're short and sarcastic all the time. You've been withdrawn and are clearly not happy. What happened over there? Did someone hurt you? Are you working through some sort of pain? We can—"

"There's nothing any of you can do," Reynard interrupted. "I'm fine."

"No, you're not," Albert said gently. "That's pretty clear. So I'll ask again, what's going on? Did you meet someone over there? Is that what happened?"

Reynard sighed. "It doesn't really matter what happened. You became ill, and I returned because I knew what my duty was. Not that you getting sick changed anything. I was going to have to leave anyway. All that happened was that I came home a few days earlier. I just need to be involved with something to help keep me occupied."

"So is that what this garden is?" Albert asked.

Reynard shook his head. "When I was in America, I met some amazing people. I don't even know her full name. I just called her Gran. She was a gardener and had turned her backyard into a paradise. I helped her do some of the heavy work, and I found it very satisfying. She showed me what you can get working with your hands as well as your mind and eyes."

Albert cleared his throat. "You know we had a grandmother."

"Who came to visit us once a week for an hour or so on a regular schedule," Reynard interjected. He had seen how people who truly cared for each other behaved, and it wasn't through formal, scheduled visits. "But that isn't the point. She wasn't my grandmother."

Albert smiled, leaning forward. "No. But she is the gran of someone." There were times when Albert could really see things clearly. It was his superpower and one of the reasons he would make a great king. Albert was a no-BS kind of guy, and he could see through a mountain of diplomatic speak to get to the nugget at the heart of a matter with ease. That sort of thing always gave Reynard a headache. "And what is this guy to you?"

"I liked him, okay?" Reynard said honestly. "He's a police officer in America. I gave an interview to a reporter while I was over there, and now that reporter is following Fisher around and causing trouble for him and his grandmother. I don't know what to do about it."

Albert cleared his throat. "And what did you do to meet this police officer?" The tone set Reynard's teeth on edge.

"I was driving too fast. Then my car broke down, and he directed me to a hotel, which caught fire. I didn't know what to do, and everyone else had found rooms and everything was full. I couldn't get to my car, so Fisher offered a room for the night." He smiled as he remembered just what the two of them had done that same night. Things had been heated almost from the moment they met, and now it felt like a wet blanket had settled over his life. Now that he knew that heat, that passion and desire, he didn't want to be without it.

"Of course he did," Albert added with his usual skepticism.

"Why? He had no idea who I was, and neither did Gran. I was just a guy to them until that damned reporter recognized me and put a tracker on my car." Come to think of it, Harvey was more of a stalker than a reporter. Reynard had probably been stupid to say one word to him. And now he was afraid the guy was never going to give up.

"So he just offered you a place to stay?"

Reynard nodded. "They were nice, and Fisher was…." He stopped himself before he went into too much detail. "Let's just say he was the male version of Contessa du Monde." Albert had had his eye on her for years. He had even asked Lillia to marry him once, but she had demurred. Albert was still pursuing her, and Reynard hoped that she would agree to marry him soon. They were perfect together. But Lillia was a private person, and she wasn't sure she wanted the royal spotlight. That alone made her even more perfect for Albert, in Reynard's opinion.

"I see."

"Yes, and he's back in the States, and I'm here because I know what my duty is. No matter what the rest of the family thinks. I just wanted the chance to be free of—" He was interrupted by a knock on the door, followed by Langley coming inside. "The fact the everyone thinks a quick knock is appropriate before they barge in," he added more loudly before turning to Langley. "Can it wait ten minutes?" Langley backed out of the room and closed the door. "My time was my own, and I got to know real people. I helped his grandmother in her garden most days, and Fisher and I went to an amusement park with huge roller coasters. I rode them all." He added in a whisper, "It was exhilarating, and I want to do it again." His excitement waned as quickly as it rose. "But it won't happen. I know that."

Albert gave him the look that would serve him well as king, part stare and part entreaty. It enticed people to speak. "And you want to see Fisher again?"

"I miss him the way you miss Lillia… only maybe more, because I doubt I'll ever see him again. I know that."

"Then just get over it."

Reynard met Albert's gaze with one even harder. "I could say the same thing to you about Lillia. But you have your heart set on her. I know you do. The last time she came to dinner, you two heated up the room to the point I needed a fan and a can of perfume to keep the pheromones at bay. Well, I feel the same way about him." He swallowed hard. Reynard hadn't meant to share all that with Albert. It just came out.

Albert nodded slowly. "Then there's only one thing you can do." Reynard waited for his brother to tell him to get over it again. "Win the man over." He said it like it was the most natural thing in the world. "Invite him to visit, show him around, and court him."

"Is that what you did with Lillia?" Reynard asked.

Albert grinned even brighter. "When I was sick, she came to me every day and even stayed with me for hours, holding my hand. I knew she was there, and when I finally felt better, she told me that she knew what she wanted now. So last night I asked her to marry me, and she agreed. It hasn't been announced, and we're going to wait to do that until I'm fully on my feet. So yes, I think a little persistence worked out." He leaned back and closed his eyes. It was clear he was tiring. "This life, one of public service, isn't easy, and it's even harder alone. So find yourself a partner, someone who will stand by you, and if he happens to be a police officer from the States… well…."

"You know how our parents are going to feel about something like that." For as long as he could remember, his parents had hammered home that their choice of partner wasn't just about them but the image of the country, and reflected on the entire family too.

"So what?" Albert said. "We deserve some happiness. And I'm starting to understand that we're at our best when we're happy, and it shows to others as well."

"Certainly, but you know that by tradition, Father has to give his blessing to anyone we wish to be with." He purposely didn't say *marry*, because legally, that area was a little murky. Veronia had been a leader in marriage equality, but royal marriage laws were a separate issue and their wording was old-fashioned, so it wasn't clear if marriage equality applied to them.

"Deal with that when the time comes," Albert suggested as another knock sounded on the door. Albert asked them to come in.

"Prince Franz, there is a guest waiting for you in the hall. I only admitted him because he said he spoke with you when you were away and that you had agreed to speak with him again. I believe he's some sort of reporter." Langley didn't pull a face, but his facial muscles twitched slightly, though he refrained from vocalizing the opinion that was clear otherwise. "He said his name was Harvey Weston."

"Thank you. Is someone with him?"

"Yes. Two of the palace guards are in the room with him. I didn't think he should be left alone."

"Very well. I'll be down to see him shortly." Reynard thought there was no harm in making him wait. Langley left the room, and Reynard said goodbye to his brother. "Congratulations again on winning Lillia. I'm happy for you, and I'll say nothing until the formal announcement." He shared a smile with his brother before leaving the room.

Langley joined him as he descended to the ground level and through the formal rooms to the entrance hall, where Harvey sat stiffly in one of the small reception chairs.

"Your Highness," Harvey said as he stood.

"Why are you here?" Reynard asked, not extending his hand. "I already gave you your story." He turned to Langley and then back to the reporter. He wasn't happy with Harvey, especially for bothering Fisher and Gran, yet he didn't want to let on that he knew what he had been up to.

"You said that if I treated you right, you'd possibly give me another story," Harvey said as some of his confidence ebbed.

"I said I might," Reynard snapped. "And coming here to try to push in to get a story isn't helping you. If I have something for you, I'll have someone call." He glanced at the guards and then the door before leaving the hall. He knew what Harvey had been doing, and he had no intention of rewarding him. Knowing the guards would see Harvey out and off the property, he didn't even look back. Instead he climbed the impressive stairs to his suite to get ready for his meeting.

"THAT SEEMS like a lot of progress," Reynard said hours later, bringing the planning session and meeting to a close.

"Do you really think we can secure permission from His Majesty?" Lenoir Genovese asked as others gathered their papers and notes.

"I hope so, yes. What the king asked for were detailed plans, and we've come a great deal closer to that today." He smiled at all of them. "We now know the scope of what we want to do, as well as an approximate cost. With royal patronage, I'm confident we can raise the money we need without public funding." He put away his own papers and the computer he'd been using to take additional notes. After thanking each member personally for their support and time, he excused himself before going upstairs to his suite.

"How was your meeting?" Langley asked as he came out of Reynard's dressing room.

"It went very well." He sat down and pulled off his shoes. "I think the planning is really coming together." He sat back and closed his eyes, an image of Fisher immediately filling his head. When he was busy, he was fine, but as soon as he slowed down, he missed the man like a limb. Maybe Albert was right and he needed to issue an invitation in order to get Fisher here so they could figure out if there was any possible way forward.

"Sir, you need some new shirts," Langley told him. "The ones you have are becoming worn. Would you like me to order some more?"

"No, I think I'm going to go into the city, and I'll visit the tailors. I want to get out anyway. A drive will help clear my head." He changed into trainers and grabbed the keys to his BMW coupe.

"Very good." Langley seemed drawn, with dark circles under his eyes, and Reynard paused.

"Are you feeling all right?" he asked.

Langley paused and blushed. "It's nothing you need be concerned about." Reynard debated pushing the issue and held Langley's gaze. "I have an appointment with a physician on Friday."

"Go now if you aren't feeling well. Drop my name if you need to, but go. I can take care of myself for the rest of the day. Look after yourself." He tried to remember the last time Langley hadn't been there whenever he'd needed something. The man was always available, and Reynard had never really given him much thought. That needed to change—*he* needed to change the way he thought of others. "Please."

"Thank you, sir," Langley said and left the suite. Reynard followed him down the hall but diverged at the stairs, where Reynard hurried out to the garage and slipped into his car. He pulled out and down the palace drive toward the gates, which opened before him, and then he was off, hitting the accelerator, the car taking the corners with ease.

He loved this drive down the hill toward the town. The curves were perfect for this car, tight and intense. He sped up, zipping toward the capital city of Constance. It was named after a much-loved queen, the wife of one of Reynard's ancestors. He reached the edge of the small city and headed toward the center of town.

Everyone knew him and his entire family here. Reynard understood that there was no anonymity. His car was known, and people waved when he pulled to a stop at a traffic signal. Others stopped to watch as he passed. When the light changed, he continued on, weaving through the old, winding city streets to the historic commercial center.

Veronia had been spared large-scale damage in the wars, so many of the historic buildings still stood, some leaning higgledy-piggledy from hundreds of years of settling. He found the shop he wanted and parked right out front.

"Your Highness," Bradford said as he hurried out of the shop. His family had owned Carrea Tailors for generations, and they proudly displayed their royal warrant in the window. "How can I help you?" The slight middle-aged man gave a small bow.

"Langley said I needed some shirts."

"You didn't need to come. An order could have been placed," he said gently. "I could have sent anything you needed to the palace." He opened the door, and Reynard went inside and locked the door behind them.

"Of course you could, but I needed some time outside." He waited while Bradford took Reynard's order.

"I heard about your project," Bradford said. "I think it's a good idea. Something to add to the city for all of us." He finished up his notes.

"Thank you." Reynard found himself watching the flow of people as they passed by the shop, some of them stopping to look at the car before moving on. Men, women, children... Fisher?

Reynard's heart stopped, and he blinked, but the man was gone. It had to be his imagination, but before he could stop himself, he was at the door and unlocked it. He rushed out onto the sidewalk and raced in the direction he thought he'd seen the man go. Looking both ways, he didn't see him. Maybe it truly had been wishful thinking.

He was about to return to the shop when the people on the walk seemed to part and Reynard saw him standing in front of the patisserie window. He would know that profile anywhere.

"Your Highness, is everything all right?" Bradford asked from behind him.

Reynard didn't dare turn away from Fisher. It was hard to believe he was here, and yet his heart raced and the air around him grew heavy. "Yes, thank you," he answered, his gaze glued to Fisher. Then he took his first steps toward him.

CHAPTER 14

THAT VOICE. It carried over the others around him, cutting through the sounds of the city and the people on the street. He knew it. Hell, for weeks Fisher had heard it in his dreams and whenever he closed his eyes. Fisher opened his mouth to say something but couldn't find his voice.

At first he stood still, his legs unable to move. Then he managed to take a few steps closer. Fisher didn't know what to do, though he wanted to crush Reynard into a hug and hold him tight. He didn't dare, though, leaving his arms to his sides as his hands tingled.

"Your Highness?" the small man behind Reynard asked.

"I know him," Reynard said without looking away. The heat between them built, just like it had back in Pennsylvania. Fisher drew even closer, and then Reynard motioned with his head and turned back toward the shop he'd come out of. Fisher followed, because the thought of not seeing Reynard again hurt like hell.

Once they were in the shop, the man locked the door behind them, and Reynard lost most of his stiffness. "What are you doing here? How long have you been here? Why didn't you come to the palace?" The questions came fast and furious.

"I got in this morning and checked into a hotel. I was out looking for something to eat, and then I intended to try to find out if you'd see me." He bit his lower lip. "I didn't know if I should come or not. I thought about messaging, but then I didn't know what your answer would be." He swallowed hard, almost unable to believe he was looking at Reynard.

"Excuse me," the small man said and went through a door to the back.

"I can hardly believe it's you," Reynard told him. "I was thinking about trying to go back to see you, and then here you are. You came all this way."

Fisher nodded slowly. "I had to. All the guys I work with told me that if I sat around moping any longer, they weren't going to speak to me again, and Gran kept giving me the stink eye." He managed a smile because Reynard was right there, though he didn't dare touch him. He thought there were rules about things like that, though Fisher wasn't sure what they were.

"So you just hopped on a plane?" Reynard asked. "I'm glad you did." His eyes grew wide, and that smile—the one Fisher had missed seeing—lit up the shop. "I just can't believe it." Before Fisher knew what was happening, Reynard had him in a hug. The dam burst, and Fisher embraced Reynard, inhaling that now-familiar scent as he tightened his hold.

"I had to try to see you again," Fisher said. "I couldn't stay there and…." His throat ached. Fisher closed his eyes, just holding on in case this was all some kind of dream and he was going to wake up at any second to empty arms.

"I'm glad you came," Reynard said softly.

A knock on the shop window had the two of them breaking apart. Reynard huffed and stood straight. Heat rose in Fisher's cheeks as he turned to see a couple of kids peering inside. He met their gaze, smiling, and they went on.

"Sorry if I've caused you trouble," Fisher said softly.

"It's pretty well known here what my preferences are." Fisher noticed that Reynard kept his distance. "But I suppose the two of us making out in public probably isn't the best idea." He smiled and then took Fisher's hand.

The small man returned. "Is there anything else, Your Highness?" he asked.

"Fisher, this is Bradford," Reynard said. "He's an amazing tailor and makes all my clothes." He stepped back, and Fisher shook Bradford's hand. He seemed a little surprised at the gesture but smiled. Fisher didn't understand the reaction.

"Here, men often embrace lightly when meeting. Shaking hands is an American greeting," Reynard said just loudly enough for Fisher to hear. Then, to Bradford, "Can you arrange to have everything delivered to the palace?"

Fisher swallowed when he realized what he was doing. Back home it had been easy for Fisher to see Reynard as just another guy. But here, with the "Your Highnesses" and the talk of palaces, it hit Fisher much harder just who Reynard was.

"Of course," Bradford said before unlocking the door. Fisher and Reynard stepped out onto the sidewalk, and Bradford stayed in the doorway.

"Do you want to look around?" Reynard asked. When Fisher nodded, Reynard led him down the sidewalk. "This is the historic center of town," Reynard explained as they strolled past buildings that seemed hundreds of years old. "The city grew out from here over the last few centuries and gets progressively newer."

"I noticed that as I came in from the airport. As I rode, I saw signs for something called an Ermine Works. What are you doing? I kept imagining rows of the little creatures on treadmills, generating power."

Reynard chuckled, and others on the street turned to watch. It seemed that even though people kept their distance, they were watching him. Or maybe they were looking to ensure that Fisher didn't do anything to their prince. He wasn't quite sure.

"The kingdom used to raise ermines. Royal garments are often trimmed with it." Reynard shook his head. "We still have some in the kingdom, but we don't harm them. They're our mascots, in a way. The ermine works is a workshop that produces artificial ermine. It looks natural, but no animals are harmed. We sell our product all over the world. It's highly specialized, and the end product is beautiful. We also produce a number of other faux-fur products as well. They are all high-quality for people who want the look of fur without harming any animals." He seemed proud, and Fisher liked that idea.

"What else do you make here?" Fisher asked, looking around at the various buildings.

"The country has a lot of artisans. We have encouraged traditional crafts and skills to continue. Masters conduct classes, and we incentivize people to take up traditional occupations. It brings continuity, and it encourages tourism. We don't have cheap trinkets made in Asia here. It's not the kind of thing we want." He pointed to a highly decorated building across a small square. "That's the artisan guild headquarters. It's a way for artists to get together and market their work collectively while promoting Veronia as a place to visit."

More people seemed to be paying attention to Reynard, and some were pointing. A few seemed like they were going to approach them. "Maybe we should get you back to your car?" Fisher said.

"That's probably not a bad idea," Reynard said softly as he waved and received greetings in return. "I feel safe here, though."

"But you don't need to cause a scene," Fisher agreed. A few groups of people followed them toward the car, and Fisher felt himself going into police mode. He watched all around, making sure everyone kept their distance and didn't pose a threat. Once Fisher got Reynard into the car, he slipped into the passenger seat.

"Do you want to take me back to my hotel?" Fisher asked once they were moving.

"That isn't necessary. You'll stay with me. We can have your things brought up," Reynard said, flashing him a grin.

Fisher swallowed hard. "You want me to stay at the palace?" he asked, wondering what the heck he was going to do in a place like that. "I'm just a police officer from Carlisle, and you want me to stay at a place like that?" Fisher could handle car chases and bringing in criminals, but the thought…. "What if I break something? Or…."

Reynard took his hand, entwining their fingers, and Fisher sighed, letting out the tension from weeks of anticipation. "There's a room that connects to mine by the dressing room. I'll have you put in there. You'll be close, and there's nothing to worry about. Yes, the palace is fancy, but in the end it's just a big home." He squeezed Fisher's fingers. "And now that you're here, I don't want to let you out of my sight."

Fisher could understand that. "I'm sort of scared that if I let you go, you'll disappear on me." Damn, he could hardly believe that he was here with Reynard, zipping along a gorgeous road. They approached a gate, and it opened for them. Reynard drove through tall trees before bursting into a clearing.

Fisher gasped at the building ahead of him. It looked like something out of a fairy tale, with a tower, a few turrets, and a stone terrace that ran along much of the front. "I can't stay here. What am I supposed to wear? How do I act?" What the hell was he supposed to do if he met the king and queen? He inhaled deeply as Reynard pulled under a portico and got out of the car. Fisher followed because he didn't want to get lost.

"I've never been in a palace before. I feel like I should be wearing something better than jeans and a T-shirt." They stepped inside an entrance hall that took his breath away. It looked like something he would see in a movie.

"I know it's a little over the top and all, but remember, this is just trappings and decorations. Nothing more." He took Fisher's hand again. "It doesn't reflect the person on the inside. Remember what you told me? Just be myself. Well, I've been trying to do that, and I want you to do the same."

"Franz," a woman said from the top of the stairs. She was small and petite, but her presence commanded the entire room. "Who is this?" She glided down the stairs with so little effort she could have been a ghost.

"Mother, this is Fisher Bronson. Fisher, I'd like to present my mother," Reynard said.

"Your Majesty," Fisher said, and bowed slightly because he didn't know what else to do.

"It's nice to meet you," she said, standing about six feet away. "My son has told me the nice things you did for him while he was running away." Her eyes blazed for just a second, and then the fire was gone, instantly doused by her polite exterior.

"We all need the chance to escape our lives sometimes. Otherwise how do we learn what's really important?" Fisher said honestly. He felt he needed to stick up for Reynard. "He may have gone away, but he came home when he was needed."

She glanced at Reynard and then back at him with eyes Fisher was sure were taking the measure of him with each passing second. "I suppose you could be right. Time will tell."

Fisher stood upright, his shoulders back, the way he had been taught in the academy. Yes, this was Reynard's mother and a queen, but he was not going to be intimidated. Everything around him was designed to do just that, and he was damned well not going to fall into the trap. "Your son is a good man. He spent a week working in the yard with my grandmother, and let me tell you, Gran is a good judge of character. When his hotel caught fire, Reynard helped people get out and then stayed back and let everyone else find a place before he got one for himself."

Concern flashed through her eyes, but it too was covered up. "Maybe the little trip was what he needed. It still wasn't kind of him to worry his father and me."

Suddenly Fisher felt like he was in a sparring match. "My gran worries about me all the time. I'm a police officer, and I know she worries every time I go to work, and she's concerned about me because I'm here. Gran raised me after my parents died, and she'll always worry, but she never held me back and always encouraged me to follow my heart." He glanced at Reynard, whose mouth hung open slightly, his eyes filled with near shock. "Parents will always be anxious about their children, but that doesn't mean they shouldn't let them go to follow their dreams."

"Even if those dreams aren't right for them?" the queen asked.

Fisher saw the trap and sidestepped it. "How do you know what Reynard's or anyone else's dream should be?" Fisher figured he had said enough.

The queen met his gaze, and then her lips curled upward just a little before she turned to Reynard. "I assume you have invited him to stay at the palace."

"Yes," Reynard said, and the queen nodded.

"Please excuse me, Mr. Bronson." She continued across the hall, her heels clicking on the stone floor before she disappeared around a corner.

Fisher thought his knees would give out. Reynard smacked him on the shoulder. "Dang. That was impressive."

"I hope she doesn't hate me," Fisher said as Reynard took his hand and led him up those grand stairs.

"Are you kidding? I think Mom liked you. Not many people would give her a run for her money, and you stood toe-to-toe with her and didn't give an inch. That was impressive." He smiled and led him up a second set of stairs and down the hall before entering a comfortable yet still impressive room with dark paneling and landscapes filling some of the eye-level wall panels. "This is my sitting room."

A knock had Fisher turning around as a man entered. "Your Highness."

"Langley, you remember Fisher Bronson. I stayed with him and his gran when I was in the States. He came to pay me a visit. Could you arrange to get his things from his hotel and put him in the adjoining room?"

"Of course," Langley said.

Fisher held out his hand, and Langley shook it firmly. "It's good to see you again." He flashed his best smile. "And thank you for your help."

"Of course, sir," Langley said, releasing Fisher's hand. "Which hotel are you staying at?"

"The Heritage," Fisher answered, and Langley made a quick note before turning to Reynard. "I need to remind you about the dinner with your family this evening, and you have a full calendar tomorrow."

"Postpone what you can for the next few days. I want to have time with Fisher, and I'd like to show him the vision for my project. Could you find out if Lenoir would be available sometime tomorrow to join us?" Reynard settled in one of the chairs.

"I'll do what I can." He headed to the door before clearing his throat. "Is Mr. Bronson joining you for dinner?"

"Yes," Reynard answered.

"Very well." He left the room, closing the door behind him.

"Are you crazy? I can go to town and get something to eat. I can't have dinner with the king and queen." The thought frightened him, but he refused to let it show.

"Why not?" Reynard asked. "They're people just like anyone else."

Fisher snorted, then covered his nose with his hand. "Please. I'm a police officer from Carlisle. I eat fast so I can get back to work. I don't know how to sit at a royal table and eat with my pinkie in the air or whatever it is that you do. And you say that your mother liked me, but I think she couldn't wait to get the heck out of there."

Reynard chuckled. "First thing, my mother never sticks around where she doesn't want to. Second, she sparred with you, and you gave as good as you got. That says a lot. And because Albert isn't up to his full strength, it's just going to be a family meal, not a state dinner. Langley is already arranging a place for you, and everyone will be polite and nice to you." He stepped back. "Now, the one thing we need is something for you to wear. Jeans won't do, and I know nothing I have will fit you." Reynard made a call and was soon speaking to Bradford. "We need your assistance. The friend who was with me today has been invited to our family dinner." Reynard listened. "That's perfect. His shoes are black trainers, and they'll have to do, but the rest would be perfect. Thank you. Send them to the palace to Langley's attention." He hung up.

"I take it Bradford is coming to my rescue?" Fisher asked, wondering how much this was going to cost. It had strained his budget to come here. Fisher made a decent salary, but he also helped Gran each month so she could stay in her home.

"Yes. He'll send some clothes over that should fit. The man is talented enough that he could approximate your size well enough for a single dinner." Reynard motioned to a chair, and Fisher sat. He felt like he had been caught in a whirlwind and had no idea how to get out of it. "I'm glad you're here."

"Me too. It's good to see you. I was trying to figure out how I was going to get to see you. I didn't think I could just come up and knock on the palace door."

"Why not? Our reporter friend certainly did," Reynard said. "I sent him packing, especially after what you told me he'd done to you and Gran."

"Yeah. Well, he's still here. I saw him lurking around downtown, talking to locals. He was asking about you and what people think of you. He has this real issue with you being gay. All his questions surrounded the topic, like he was trying to dig up some juicy gossip. As far as I could hear, no one told him anything, but you never know. I stayed away from him and hoped he didn't recognize me." Fisher could only imagine the gossip he'd make of Fisher being here.

Reynard leaned forward, taking Fisher's hands. "I can think of a lot more interesting things to talk about than Harvey." He smiled, heat filling his eyes. "I've thought about you a great deal."

Fisher swallowed under his intense gaze. "Me too."

He glanced at the door and then back to Reynard as he got off the chair and drew close, sliding his hands up Fisher's arms and then around his back. "I was never able to give you a proper welcome." Before Fisher realized it, Reynard's lips were inches from his. "I missed you so much."

Fisher nodded. "Me too. But can we do this here?" He had already seen people knock and walk in. "What if someone sees?"

"Then they will leave the room and pretend they didn't," Reynard said.

Fisher snorted again. "And if they find us on the floor, getting busy?"

"Then they will say nothing, and no one will ever just come in again," Reynard said with a smirk. "If you want, we could test that theory."

"I don't think so." Still, Fisher kissed Reynard hard, taking what he had been thinking about so many times when he'd been alone. His body stirred to flame almost instantly, and Fisher was so damned tempted to press Reynard down on the sofa and take what he wanted. Every instinct that had been denied for weeks screamed at him to make love to Reynard, but he had to hold back. Reynard tasted amazing, though, and Fisher couldn't seem to get enough. He cupped his head, holding him as he deepened the kiss, sending his mind whirring.

There was a knock, and then the door opened. Fisher pulled back, but by the time he turned, the door was closing once again. "See?"

Reynard kissed him again, and Fisher stood and lifted Reynard off his feet. "Bedroom," he growled, and Reynard tilted his head to the side. That was enough to show Fisher the direction, and he walked the two of them that way and into a sumptuous room that barely registered in Fisher's consciousness.

He reached the bed and lifted Reynard up on it. "Damn, I want you. I've lain awake nights wishing you were next to me, and now I'm here with you and I'm nervous."

Reynard stroked his cheeks. "Why?"

"Because what if I'm making more of things than there was? What if the king walks in and sees me going at it hammer and tongs with his son?" He suppressed a giggle, and Reynard rolled his eyes.

"Sir," a voice called from the other room, and Fisher pulled away from Reynard's radiant warmth.

"I guess you and I will have to wait until tonight when everyone else is in bed." He nuzzled the base of Reynard's neck. "I do hope that no one in the palace is expecting a quiet night." He winked, and Reynard climbed off the bed and went into the other room. Fisher followed behind.

"Your luggage has been brought to your room, and some clothes have been sent over for you for dinner," Langley said a little stiffly. His expression remained bland, but his eyes were another matter. Fisher read people all the time, and there was something off about Langley. Maybe he was just protective of Reynard, and for that Fisher couldn't blame him. He could imagine that there were plenty of people who would try to take advantage of him. Fisher wasn't one of them.

"Thank you." He looked down and realized his clothes were mussed and it looked exactly like he and Reynard had been rolling around together.

"That will be all for now. I'll see that Fisher is ready for dinner," Reynard said gently.

"Very good." Langley left the room and closed the door behind him.

"He's kind of intense," Fisher commented.

Reynard nodded. "Langley has been my assistant for years now. He's had to put up with a lot. I was quite the rebel for many years."

"You? No," Fisher mugged, and they both laughed. "I can imagine you gave him a run for his money. I'm surprised he didn't leave."

"He threatened to about five years ago. I was pretty wild and wouldn't listen to anyone. Albert helped me understand that I could either fight who I was or figure out a way to live with it." He sighed and sat down on the sofa. "I'm still figuring out the second part." Fisher took a place next to him. "There are times when I like being a prince, but then there are the instances when it's all about me behaving a certain way and putting on a show of unity or something. And I don't have anything official to do. Albert has a role because he's the heir, and I'm just expected to stand quietly in the background, smile, and nod."

"Well, I think you do more than that. People were talking about your park garden project, and they like it. You saw how people reacted to you. They smiled and seemed to like you. I only heard a few people talking in one of the shops, but I think people see you as the approachable royal. And maybe that's good. They certainly weren't keen to talk to Harvey." How in the hell did their conversation get back here again? Fisher stroked Reynard's cheek and drew closer.

There was something about Reynard that took his breath away, and Fisher loved that feeling. It was like the best drug ever, and damn it all, but he was hopelessly addicted. Reynard had the most amazing eyes, and if he looked closely, he could see Reynard's doubts and fears. He didn't think most people could, but Fisher definitely did. "You don't need to hide yourself from me."

Reynard leaned forward slowly until their foreheads touched. "I know. It's just that I'm used to hiding. It's part of the job."

Fisher smiled. "Yeah. Except as you've said, you don't have one. Not officially anyway. So use that fact to make things better for people."

"Excuse me?" Reynard said.

"There are police officers who have retired from the force. Some of them become private investigators or security specialists. They work for who they want and take the cases that interest them. They don't need to do what a captain or someone else tells them to do." Fisher gathered Reynard close. "Your brother is bound by centuries of tradition. I bet that includes the type of person he has to marry and how he is expected to act. Right?"

Reynard nodded. "He needs to marry someone of noble birth, and he's lucky there because he fell in love with Lillia. She's everything the family could want… and Albert adores her."

"But you can follow your own path." He smiled. "You have an education, and you're smart. So find a career of your own. Make your own way." Fisher swallowed. "I've been giving this some thought. You say your family wants to run too much of your life, so make your own."

"You mean like the garden?"

Fisher shook his head. "I love that idea, and it's using your position to help others. But I'm saying get yourself a job and make your own way." Reynard seemed shocked. "I don't mean work in a shop or anything, but find your own means of supporting yourself. Make a life outside of your family."

"I've thought of that, but do you know how nearly impossible it is? Anything I do would be seen as banking on my name and position as prince. Companies would want to hire me or do business with me because of who I am. And I can't put my family in that kind of position. Anything that's done or anyone who does business with me would be looked at under a microscope… and so would I." Reynard grew quiet. "But you are right in a way. What I need to do is create a place for myself within the family."

"And how do you do that?"

Reynard smiled. "I think I've already started. Tomorrow I want to show you what I have planned and what the team I've put together is working on." He seemed so excited, and Fisher liked that Reynard might have found a path for himself.

A knock on the door paused their conversation. Fisher stifled a groan. Did anyone ever get to finish a conversation around here without someone interrupting?

"Yes?" Reynard said without pulling away.

"Dinner is in an hour," Langley reminded them.

"Thank you," Reynard answered, and the door closed without Langley so much as peering inside.

Clearly he was a little afraid of what he was going to see. "He's probably waiting just outside the door."

Fisher pulled away. "And I should probably get dressed." After a final longing look, he left the room.

Langley was indeed in the hall, and he showed Fisher to the luxurious room next to Reynard's. It was fit for a prince, and Fisher was afraid to touch anything. God, this was so not his life. He wondered once more what he was doing here and how he thought he could be a part of Reynard's life. It was all too much—they were so different. Fisher wasn't some character in a fairy tale, and he shouldn't let himself get carried away.

CHAPTER 15

REYNARD KNOCKED on Fisher's door, then opened it when he answered. He stepped inside as Fisher came out of the bathroom. "Your friend sure knows what he's doing."

He had to agree with Fisher. The shirt fit beautifully, and Louis had chosen a gorgeous pair of light gray slacks that almost shimmered as he moved. "He certainly does." Not to mention the man filled out the clothes in all the best ways. "You look wonderful."

"Thanks. I'm still really nervous. I've washed my hands three times to try to get them clean enough." He held them out. "I hope I look okay." He was clearly nerving himself up.

Reynard took his hand. "We have a few minutes before we need to go down." He brought Fisher to the sofa, and they sat down. "At dinner, there is no formality. This is the family. We do wait for my father, and then dinner will be served. You don't need to worry about waiting for anyone else or rush to eat. If you're in doubt about silverware, watch me or Albert. If you aren't sure, then work your way in from the outside toward the plate, though it isn't going to be that fancy. Lillia will be there, and she's a very good, down-to-earth lady."

"But what if I mess up?" Fisher asked.

"The height of manners is making a guest feel at ease, so no one should say or do anything to draw attention. Most of all, be yourself, okay? This is a family meal. My parents just happen to be king and queen, but they are my parents." He tried to reassure Fisher as best he could. "Now let's go down."

Fisher squeezed his hand, and Reynard held it in return. When Fisher eased off, Reynard retained his hold because he wanted to maintain a connection.

Just outside the dining room, he released Fisher's hand. "You look great. And do you remember the day you pulled me over? You were so confident and forceful. Be him." He smiled, and they entered. This wasn't the large state dining room, but a smaller dining area used for family meals. It was bright, with windows that looked out over the palace gardens. He and Fisher were the first to arrive, with Albert and Lillia right behind them.

Fisher nodded to each of them as Reynard made introductions. "I see you're sporting a new addition," Reynard told Lillia, admiring her engagement ring.

"Yes. He asked me this afternoon, and I accepted." She put her hand on Albert's arm, looking at him with as much adoration as Albert gave her.

"Congratulations," Fisher said warmly. "That's wonderful."

Lillia blushed slightly. She was never someone to want fame. "Thank you. I turned him down twice."

"Can I ask why?" Fisher asked. He spoke so gently to her. It was kind of sweet.

"I didn't know if I could handle being in the spotlight. Albert will be king someday, and I didn't know if I wanted that kind of attention." She turned to Albert with a radiant smile. "But he won me over." Albert put an arm around her, and Reynard took Fisher's hand just as his mother and father entered the room. Fisher stood straighter as soon as he saw them, then bowed slightly.

"You must be Fisher," his father said forcefully.

"Yes, sir," Fisher answered. "It's good to meet you." He raised his hand and then let it fall back to his side.

"It's okay to shake my father's hand. He knows what it means," Reynard whispered, and Fisher offered his hand again. Reynard smiled as his father shook it.

"I understand you're a relatively new police officer." His father's gaze was firm, and Fisher stood tall. Reynard was so proud of him. The king could be intimidating when he wanted to be.

"Yes, sir. I graduated top of my class from the state police academy and was lucky enough to be posted near where I was raised. Right now I live with my grandmother. She's the only family I have left." Reynard squeezed Fisher's fingers and then released them.

"You live with her?" Reynard's mother asked.

"Yes, ma'am. Gran is getting older, and I want her to be able to stay in her own home. She and I have separate schedules. She has her garden club and other activities, and I have work and friends. But she helps take care of me, and I do the same for her. After my mother died, she and Gramps took me in. They put their retirement on hold so they could raise me. I'm only returning the care she showed me." The conviction in his voice raised the temperature in the room. "And just so there is no confusion, I care for your son."

"You understand that his mother and I are dubious of anyone in our children's lives," his father said as he took his place at the end of the table.

"Of course I do. Just like Gran is for me. She looked Reynard over from head to toe like the grand dame lion she is. And the two of them bonded in her garden." Damn, the smile he sent Reynard's way was radiant. "I believe in honesty and being up-front. I didn't know that Reynard was a prince until he started being followed."

"Reynard?" his father asked.

"That's the name I used."

Fisher turned to him. "And I like it."

"That was my father's name," his mother said.

"It's how I think of you," Fisher told him. "I don't see Prince Franz… or anyone other than the man who helped an old couple out of a burning hotel and then let everyone else find a place after the hotel fire before worrying about himself. That's Reynard."

His mother cleared her throat. "That's all well and good. But what are your plans?" She sipped from her glass as appetizer plates with three bite-size savories in pastry were placed in front of each of them. "I'm assuming that you can't leave your grandmother and that this is just a visit."

"I don't really know, ma'am," Fisher said. "I came here to see Reynard, and I hoped that we could talk. Since he left, I've missed him, and I really came here to try to get some sort of closure. Maybe if I saw him again, I could get him out of my system and move on."

"That seems sensible."

Reynard was about to interject before his mother went on, but Fisher squeezed his leg lightly. "It does. And the last thing I expected was to be having dinner with all of you. I just wanted to talk to Reynard, but seeing him…."

"I think it's wonderful," Lillia said with a smile.

Clearly Reynard's parents didn't agree with her sentiment. "Mother, Father, I like Fisher. He's real, and he looks at the world from a different perspective. He wasn't raised the way we were, and he hasn't had the easiest life."

"Son—"

"Father," he pressed. "Fisher is important. I want to spend more time with him to see if things might develop." He turned to Lillia and Albert in their bubble of happy bliss. "I want what they have, and I deserve it. Joining this family is hard, and I don't know if Fisher is willing to take on what's required to join us. But I want to find out if there's chance. Can you understand that?" He pushed his plate slightly away, his appetite having left him.

"What will the people of Veronia and the press say if we announce that the two of you are…?" His father's words faltered. "I don't even know what to call the two of you together."

"Sir, the term would be *partners* and eventually *husbands*," Fisher supplied. "I know this is a lot for you to take in, and this hasn't happened yet. Nothing has, other than Reynard and I trying to figure things out. Maybe this is all for naught. I know he can't leave Veronia without creating a great deal of talk and bringing unwanted attention. And I have Gran that I have to think about. It isn't just me. Besides, Reynard and I haven't known each other that long. I just hope that you'll give us a chance."

Reynard watched his parents glance at one another, the silent communication he'd seen since childhood happening before his eyes. Sometimes he swore they could read each other's minds. "Very well. Your mother and I want both our children to be happy. And goodness knows this life isn't as easy as some would think. It's a public life that puts every decision, every action, out in the public spotlight. And you need someone who can support you." His father patted his mother's hand. "Someone who will always be there no matter what, because doing this job for forty years takes a great deal of strength and help." He then turned to Fisher. "But this life isn't for everyone, and anyone who enters into it lightly often regrets it and then finds they can't back out." That flint hardness in his eyes told Reynard a lot, and he saw and felt the tension rise from Fisher.

"Thank you," Reynard said to his parents.

"I appreciate that," Fisher said. "Is this how meals usually are? I feel like I'm in the hot seat."

"Sometimes," Albert said. "Both Franz and I have had people who have tried to work their way into our lives just because of who we are and who our parents are. It's something we have to be conscious of."

Fisher nodded his understanding.

"This is a family dinner, and we talk about things that are important," his father said. "Duty comes first, and it's part of the fabric of our lives. I don't doubt that you care for our son. But I don't think you have any idea what being with him entails. I don't think he truly does either." His father, having made his pronouncement, began slowly eating his canapés. Reynard knew that Fisher had to be about ready to run for the hills.

"Have you ever been shot at in your work? I hear there are lots of guns where you live," Lillia asked, probably trying to change the subject.

Reynard wanted to kiss her for it. She really was going to make a good partner for Albert.

"No. I had a suspect point a gun at me once, but my patrol partner was able to help defuse the situation. I've had to pull my gun a few times, but I have never shot at someone. Most of the guys say it's only a matter of time, but I hope it's later rather than sooner." He sipped his wine, and Reynard did the same. "What sort of work do you do?"

"Lillia is a researcher. She's working on her PhD in art history, and it's our plan to try to build up Veronia as an art and culture destination. We're close to France and in the heart of Europe, but very few people really know about us, so we think we can help craft an image." Albert grinned. "And your garden idea works perfectly with that."

Fisher bumped Reynard's shoulder.

"Is there something going on between you two?" Reynard's mother asked.

"I'm working on plans for the garden and arboretum, and I showed some of them to Albert."

"They're going to be impressive," Albert said.

"Reynard is going to take me over to look at the proposed site tomorrow, and I'm really interested. Gran would love to be part of this kind of project," Fisher said gently. "It's really what she loves."

Reynard smiled to himself as an idea formed in the back of his mind.

"She would adore being part of that," Fisher added, surprising Reynard. Even his parents paused with bites halfway to their mouths. "Gran loves New York. When I was a teenager, she took me to my first live theater. *Sunset Boulevard*. I adored it." He continued speaking to Albert, but Reynard saw how his parents took in every word. "She and I go just about every year. I've been to the Met and the Cloisters, as well as the Lauder, the Frick, and I've viewed the collection at the public library. Gran took me everywhere. I know I'm a cop and most people don't think I'd like things like that, but Gran showed me how important it was. On our last trip, we did the MOMA and the Guggenheim. We last went a few months ago."

"You're an art lover," Lillia said, setting aside her fork.

"I never studied it, but I know what I like. I think that art and theater show us aspects of being human that we can't necessarily experience ourselves. At least that's how Gran explained it to me, and I agree with her. She's an artist in a way. She uses plants, and her garden is her canvas. So I think what you want to do is wonderful. Just do it differently from everyone else."

"How so?" Reynard's father interjected.

"Well…." Some of Fisher's confidence seemed to falter. "Cannes has its film festival and all that. No one can compete with Paris, London, Florence, and Rome with their collections. So don't try. I mean, you could spend a fortune on art and come up second-best, no matter what."

"What do you suggest?" Albert asked.

"That's enough. We don't need to put our guest on the spot. It isn't polite," Mother said, her manners kicking in.

"I'd really like his opinion," Albert pressed. "We're thinking the same thing that Fisher is, but we aren't sure which way to go."

Fisher turned to him, and Reynard smiled. He was fairly sure Albert wasn't leading Fisher into a trap. "Well, you could do an art fair, but not one where artists come in to sell stuff as much as where people can come to learn and experience the joy of making something or learning from others." He looked all around the table. "Could you imagine the wonder of being able to learn from Picasso when he was alive, or Jackson Pollock? I don't know if it would work, but…."

Lillia grinned. "A fair to encourage and help find the next generation of artists." She put her hands together, beaming at Albert. "I love it. With royal patronage and sponsorship, this could be a real contribution to the world. And it wouldn't be just for art per se, but film, poetry—all the things that make the world brighter." She smiled at Fisher and reached across the table to tap his hand. "I think that is a brilliant idea." She continued beaming as the next course was brought.

Fortunately, the rest of dinner was more subdued with more normal conversation and Fisher out of the hot seat. After the napoleons for dessert were finished, they all left the table. Reynard's parents went up to their sitting room.

"Would you like to join us on the terrace?" Albert asked, and the four of them headed out. One of the servants wheeled out a bar cart and then left without a word.

"How do they know what to do?" Fisher asked, watching as the door closed behind the man.

"Sometimes we arrange things ahead of time, but this is something Lillia and I do quite often after dinner, so the staff is ready for it." Albert sat down, offering Fisher a seat. Lillia sat next to him on the wicker settee. "It may not look like it, but a lot of our lives are routine. The king and queen often go to their room in the evening. They lead very public lives with a lot of engagements, so these few hours are generally theirs to spend together. The staff know that, and drinks and most likely some chocolates will be waiting for them."

"I see. But don't things get boring?" Fisher asked, his gaze going to each of them.

"Not at all," Lillia said. "There are plenty of royal duties, and they can be unpredictable sometimes. So the time here with the family is for recharging." She held Albert's hand. "And we all need that."

Fisher nodded.

"Have we scared you off yet?" Reynard asked Fisher, hoping that dinner hadn't been too much.

Fisher shrugged. "I don't know. I get the feeling that dinner was some kind of test, and I don't know if I passed or not."

Albert put his head back, laughing. Then he held out his hand. "You owe me twenty euros," he told Lillia, who had the grace to look embarrassed.

"What did you bet?" Fisher asked.

"I said you'd pass the test," Lillia put in hurriedly. "And you did, better than I did, I think."

"I also thought you'd pass, and I added that you'd figure it out." He practically cackled, and Reynard wasn't sure if he should be upset or not. "I thought it would take a smart man to win Reynard's heart. That and you looked determined."

"Did you know?" Fisher asked Reynard with a scowl. Albert got out of the line of fire and poured glasses of wine, then handed one to Lillia, Fisher, and finally Reynard.

Reynard nodded. "It's kind of a family thing. You bring the person you're interested in for dinner, and my parents grill them. I've only brought one other guy home, and he was out the door after dinner so fast it took the staff days to remove his tire marks from the drive."

"You not only stuck it out, but you stood toe-to-toe with the queen," Lillia said. "She nearly made me cry my first dinner here. Albert clued me in under his breath, and I made it through dinner."

"And because of that, it took me three proposals before she said yes." Albert put an arm around her shoulder in a beautiful display of affection.

"So did I pass?" Fisher asked.

Lillia raised her glass. "I'd say with flying colors." They clinked glasses, and Reynard felt like he could breathe for the first time since they sat down for dinner. Now he just had to figure out how to get Fisher to want to stay.

CHAPTER 16

WHAT THE hell was he going to do? Fisher could feel the blood rushing through his veins. He'd just had dinner with the king and queen, and now everyone was talking about duty and what it was like to join the family. He'd even managed to bumble his way through some sort of test, which he apparently passed.

"You okay?" Reynard asked as Albert and Lillia wandered to the terrace rail, looking out over the lighted formal garden like they were in some fairy tale. Maybe they were, and he was the frog.

Fisher drained the reminder of the wine and set his glass on the nearby table, tempted to ask for more, but getting drunk wasn't the answer. Hell, just one of those heated looks that Reynard was giving him right now was enough to make him feel drunk. That's what Reynard did to him, and how could he give that up?

His mind went in circles as he sat looking out over the garden. "What am I going to do?" he asked in a whisper. He didn't think he could do this. Reynard's life was so different from anything he knew. If he stayed with Reynard, he was going to be the center of everyone's attention. The crap with that damned reporter Harvey was going to seem like the opening act in a paparazzi-fueled nightmare. "I'm a private person, and I wasn't born for this."

"No one is," Lillia said. She must have overheard him. Fisher was embarrassed and wished he could just go inside and hide for a while. "We all learn how to behave in public." She still held Albert's hand as she sat down. "And you can too. Albert and Reynard were taught from birth, and so was I, to a degree. But you can learn what you need to."

That seemed like too much. Fisher wondered if it would even be possible for him to ever fit into this life. The thought of going back to the States and leaving Reynard behind left him as cold as those nights he'd spent up in his room after Reynard was gone, though, and he didn't want to go back to that. Fisher took Reynard's hand and closed his eyes, trying to stop the whirling doubts that ran through his head.

Granted, Reynard hadn't even asked him to stay, so maybe he was getting ahead of himself.

Great. Now he had something else to think about.

"Sir," a man in a dark blue uniform with gold braid on the shoulder said as he hurried up the terrace stairs. "I need to ask you to go inside. Someone has been spotted on the grounds."

"Where?" Fisher shot to his feet, bringing Reynard with him. "Go inside, all three of you." He remained calm but was ready for action. "Have the king and queen been notified?" Fisher already had Albert, Reynard, and Lillia moving toward the palace. Other guards came out from inside and got the others behind closed doors. "Where did you see him?"

"You should go inside, sir," the guard said.

"I'm a police officer," he answered. "How many were spotted, and where?" He kept his voice down.

"One. Over by the main fountain." He pointed, and Fisher headed down the stairs, staying in the shadows with the guard behind him. At the bottom, Fisher glanced around the base of the balustrade just as a shadow shifted back from the shadowed side of the huge base that surrounded the decorative water feature. Fisher pointed, and the guard—Fisher wished he knew his name—nodded and slipped back.

"Have the other guards come around from that direction," Fisher whispered. The guard nodded and spoke softly into a radio. A minute later, a figure came around the far corner of the palace, and the shadowy figure moved in their direction.

As soon as he was close enough, Fisher raced out and tackled the man to the ground.

"Watch what you're doing," the intruder groused. Fisher glared at Harvey, splayed on the ground. "You'll break the camera." He acted as though this was some sort of evening stroll.

"What the hell are you doing here sneaking onto the grounds?" Fisher growled. He wanted to pull Harvey to his feet and shake some sense into him. Instead, he held him down as the guards approached.

"You know this man?" the guard who had been with him asked.

"Yes. He's a reporter. He followed Prince Franz when he was in the States, and I've seen him here." He backed away as the regular guards took over. He wasn't sure what the laws were here, but at the very least, they had to be able to get him for breaking onto the grounds.

"They know what to do," the guard said as the others got Harvey to his feet and escorted him away. "I'm Jean Paul."

"Fisher," he said, shaking his hand.

"You are fast," Jean Paul said.

"Thanks," Fisher said with a smile. "I need to make sure the others are okay." He and Jean Paul returned to the terrace before going inside.

"Did you locate the intruder?" the king asked as soon as they entered the salon where the entire royal

family had taken refuge. Fisher couldn't help noticing
the windows that overlooked the garden and shook his
head. These people needed a great deal more security.
Not only were folks getting onto the grounds, but the
family wasn't in a secure location when there was a
threat.

"Yes, Your Majesty. Fisher stopped him," Jean
Paul said as Fisher hurried to Reynard. He had to make
sure he was fine. Even though Harvey hadn't gotten
near any of them, he certainly could have, and that had
Fisher hugging Reynard tightly, regardless of who was
watching.

"That's good," the king said. "Thank you, Jean
Paul." He left the room with the queen, and Fisher
watched Albert and Lillia over Reynard's shoulder.

"Is that it?" Fisher asked, holding Reynard tighter.
"Who is your head of security?"

"That would be Jean Paul," Albert said, and Fisher
shook his head. "Why?"

"Is he going to do a complete security assessment?
Someone got onto the palace grounds. That means they
could do it again. It was just Harvey this time, and
he was only armed with a camera, but what if it were
someone looking to harm any of you? This has to be
taken seriously."

"All right," Albert began.

"What do you think should be done?" Reynard asked.

"First thing, when there is a threat, don't go into a
room full of windows. You need to be taken to a secure
location until the threat is dealt with. If he had had a
gun…." The idea sent a chill through Fisher. "I'm sorry, this is really not my business. But you need to be
kept safe." He forced himself to stop. "I'm sure your
people know what they're doing."

Reynard patted his shoulder. "This is what I've been talking about. The king and queen are stuck in the last century. We can't keep doing things the way we have been. My parents feel that the palace guard is sufficient, and yet they're more ceremonial than efficient security."

"They could probably be both with some training," Fisher offered. "They seemed like good people who know how to work together." He was growing tired, and he stifled a yawn. This had been one hell of a day. "I think I need to rest."

"Good night," Lillia said.

"Yes. Good night, and thank you for your candidness," Albert told him before gently taking Lillia's hand and leading her out of the room.

"I'm sorry I opened my big mouth," Fisher said.

Reynard shook his head before turning out the lights. Then he cupped Fisher's cheeks and drew him closer. "You only said what you did because you care." Without another word, Reynard kissed him passionately enough that Fisher pulled him close, taking those sweet lips in a kiss that curled his toes. "I think you and I should go upstairs."

Reynard nodded, and Fisher pulled away. Then he took Fisher's hand and led him out of the room and up the grand stairs before going down the hall to their rooms. Reynard tugged Fisher into his suite and closed the door. "I've waited for this all day."

"Me too." Fisher lifted Reynard off his feet and carried him into the bedroom, his fatigue gone. "I seem to recall we were interrupted the last time we were in here."

"Yes, we were," Reynard agreed and tugged Fisher closer, but he resisted. "What's going on?"

Fisher set him on the bed and then sat next to him. "What is it you want?" Fisher asked. "I'm here, and I missed you. I know that. But is this—you and me— something you want? Because I don't know how this can work. What do I do—move here and give up my life?" He could just see himself as Reynard's arm candy, walking behind him.

"No, I don't want that for you." Reynard stroked his arm. "I guess I see you figuring out a new life for yourself. That is, if you want to stay."

Fisher sighed. "I don't know what I want. When Jean Paul said that someone was on the grounds, my first thought was to keep you safe. Then I find you in a room full of windows, and all I could think was what would have happened if it had been someone with a gun instead of just Harvey." Thinking about that alone made Fisher nervous. "I want to keep you safe, and I know that being without you sucks."

Reynard nodded. "I can't move to Carlisle. I couldn't do that to my family, and my duty is here. I know I sometimes think that everything is about me, but it really isn't. I've had advantages others could only dream about."

"You can't walk away from the money?" Fisher asked. Reynard gasped, and Fisher regretted the question. "That wasn't what I meant."

"I've had these advantages all my life, and they were paid for by my family and the people of Veronia. It would be wrong to turn my back on all that. I need to do what I can to give back. And I can't do that if I'm not here. My trip to Carlisle taught me that—I can't just turn my back. But I don't want to lose you either. I figured out what I really wanted in Carlisle, and that's you. As my father said, it's important to find someone who will be my partner."

"But I don't know if I can." Fisher paused, because he would do just about anything for Reynard—he knew that. "We've known each other a short time. It seems fast for me to think about moving here, and...." He groaned. "What? I don't have a place here, and you ran away because you didn't have one either. So what's going to happen? You and I get together, I move here, and we'll be the misfits together? You didn't have a role, and I won't either."

Reynard bounced to the edge of the bed. "That's because I didn't see it, but I do now. I kept expecting the king or my brother to give me a role. But I know now that I have to make one for myself, thanks to you. And I'm doing that. I want to head projects for the good of the people, things that they can use and enjoy every day. I want to try to make my country better for them. I have to be the one to figure out where I belong, and so do you."

Fisher understood that. He was a police officer, and Fisher would be blind to think that he couldn't make a contribution here. He knew he could. Tonight had made that obvious. "I think I just need some time to figure things out."

Reynard climbed off the bed. "I see."

Fisher tugged him back between his legs. "I don't think so. I said I needed time to think about it. That didn't mean I wanted to be alone. This place is huge, and there might be monsters under the bed." He smiled. "Someone is going to have to keep them away." He loved Reynard's smirk and the fact that he got Fisher's goofy sense of humor.

"I'm really good at that," Reynard said, drawing nearer. "I think I can do that in my sleep... or not sleeping, as the case may be." He closed the distance between them, and Fisher wound his arms around him, hugging him tightly as their lips met.

Reynard loved when they came together. He and Fisher were from different backgrounds, but here, at this moment, as Fisher stripped him naked and laid him on the bed, they were the same. Reynard loved how Fisher felt against him, and in the dark, nothing came between them. Fisher was the same as him. Yes, they came from separate worlds, but just as they joined in the dark with passion and care, they could go the same direction together in life. Reynard knew it just as clearly as he knew that Fisher completed him, filled him, and made him feel whole. Reynard knew as he looked deep into Fisher's eyes that he had found the other half of himself, and all he could hope was that Fisher felt it too.

TWO PALACE guards had checked the area over before moving away so they could have some privacy. Fisher was amazing. He had instructed the guards without actually appearing to do so, and they had both looked at Fisher with respect. Reynard could already see Fisher fitting in, even if Fisher might not see it yet.

"I don't see this as a formal place, but one with flowing beds and plenty of trees. We had a storm that brought down a lot of the older specimens about five years ago, and since then, it's grown wild. We could replant, the trees first, and then raise the money for the conservatory, which would go over there in that clearing. I'd like it to have sections so we can showcase plants native to Veronia, as well as others from other regions of the world. I'd love to have a desert garden as well as a rainforest. There are so many things we could do."

Fisher took his hand, and they stood together. "Gran would love visiting something like this." He squeezed Reynard's hand. "She always has so many more ideas than she can ever bring to life in her own garden."

"I know. She told me about some of them. Gran said she always wanted a rose garden, and I thought we'd plant one in that direction where it would get enough sun. Roses grow beautifully here, and we could bring in as many species as possible. We could also have a peony garden and a dahlia garden, among others. There are garden clubs here in Veronia, and we could see if any of them wanted to create a garden of their own. Really make this about the people and for them."

"I love that. What would you call it?" Fisher asked.

Reynard rolled his eyes. "It certainly is not going to be the 'King This' or 'Queen That' garden. No royal names. I want it to be for the people, and I don't want it to seem out of touch with them. Maybe we'll have a contest and let the people name it." He liked that idea and made a mental note to bring it up to the committee. "I also wanted to develop an event space here. Maybe for weddings or small concerts, things like that. We're still working to finalize the plans, and I don't want to try for too much."

Fisher smiled. "Why not? Plan for the brass ring. Go for everything you want and make the plans executable in stages. Then build what's truly important first, and add on additional projects." Fisher brought Reynard's hand to his lips and kissed the back of it. "I know you'll figure it out."

Reynard leaned against Fisher. Very few people had told him that he could do anything. His parents always spent more effort and time with Albert because he was the heir. Reynard had been loved and cared for, but their expectations for him were so different. All they seemed to want him to do was not embarrass the family. Which is exactly why he'd rebelled and done just that on more than one occasion. "Do you really think so?"

"Of course. This is a great undertaking, and it will make an unused area of what is now scrub land available and accessible to the public. You could even work with your brother and Lillia on their art project to incorporate that as well. Albert will support this, so you support him, and together you'll both come out on top." Reynard drew closer, and Fisher was thankful they were alone. "I'm proud of you. This is a great idea."

Reynard paused, looking surprised. Like no one had said something like that to him in a very long time. "Thank you," Reynard said as he leaned closer.

"Prince Franz!" a man called from the edge of the trees, holding a camera. The guards hurried over, and Fisher stepped in front of Reynard, instantly on edge and ready for trouble.

"What do you want?" Fisher demanded, glaring at the reporter.

"Is this man your boyfriend?" he asked.

Fisher turned to the guards. They snapped to and escorted the reporter off the grounds. However, within a minute, six other reporters stepped out of the trees, asking questions over each other. The guards released the first reporter and called for reinforcements and a car. Reynard stiffened, and Fisher knew he needed to take charge of the situation in the hope he could defuse it until backup arrived.

"Hold on," Fisher called forcefully in a deep, resonant voice filled with power. "The prince will take a few of your questions, but only if you're civil and respectful." He remained calm. Reynard nodded his agreement, and only then did Fisher step back slightly from Reynard.

"Is this man your boyfriend?" a woman asked.

Reynard turned to Fisher, his expression uncertain.

"The prince and I are figuring things out." Fisher took Reynard's hand. A few cameras went off, but Reynard simply moved closer in a show of solidarity. Fisher really liked the way Reynard stepped up and didn't try to hide. "Your prince is a wonderful man with a big heart who cares deeply about his country. The two of us are still getting to know one another, and neither of us has anything more to say about our relationship at this time."

"So there is a relationship?" the woman added, but Reynard ignored her and took another question. Fisher had said all there was to say. The next question was about why they were here, and Reynard explained about his garden idea and what he was trying to do. Fisher was pleased when the reporters picked up on the theme and asked additional questions. Some good publicity about Reynard's project could only help.

"Has the king given his blessing?"

"Not yet. He's interested, but like any good monarch, he wishes to see the detailed plans before allowing the project to go forward," Reynard said, picking up on a theme Fisher had used. He continued answering questions until more security arrived. Then they turned and headed away from the now-dispersing reporters, walking back toward the car, which was parked at the entrance road.

"How did they find us?" Reynard asked. "This area isn't currently used all that often."

Fisher climbed into the car after Reynard and settled on the back seat. "I think we have to assume that we're going to be watched whenever we're outside the palace. They are going to be looking for any sort of story now that they know the two of us are seeing each other." Fisher hated that notoriety, but he'd endure it so Reynard didn't have to go through it alone.

Reynard swore under his breath, but Fisher didn't understand him.

"It's a good thing. We didn't give them much, and they can print what they like. Gran knows I'm here, and she's the only person I'm concerned about." Fisher got on his phone and seemed to be texting back and forth. "Gran says that if anyone shows up at her house, she'll call Wyatt, and he can get them to go away." He smiled. "She also sends her love and says that if I don't treat you right then she'll paddle my backside. Apparently you and Gran got along really well."

"She and I had quite a few hours in that garden of hers, and we really got to talk." They pulled up to the palace and under the portico. Reynard got out and waited for Fisher before going inside. Langley was waiting for them inside the hall, and Fisher wondered what he wanted.

"What is it?" Reynard asked. "What message were you sent to deliver?"

"The queen has asked to speak to Fisher," Langley said.

Fisher was curious what she wanted with him. "Where is she?"

"In her study," Langley answered.

Reynard turned to Fisher and held out his hand.

"She wished to speak to him alone," Langley said in a tone that broached no argument. Reynard stepped back, and Fisher followed Langley up the stairs, wondering what Reynard's mother wanted. He turned back to where Reynard stood at the base of the stairs and flashed him a smile. Then he continued up the stairs, wondering if he was a lamb being led to the slaughter.

LANGLEY KNOCKED on the door and opened it. Fisher followed him inside. and Langley exited right away, closing the door behind him.

"Your Majesty," Fisher said, figuring this wasn't a social call. It was probably safe to be formal at a time like this.

"Fisher, please sit. I have some tea," she offered.

Fisher smiled and thanked her for the invitation before sitting in the highbacked chair offered. She handed him a cup and then sat down across from him.

"What is it you wanted?"

"I see you're direct. Good. So am I." She sipped from her cup and set it on the small table beside her. Fisher did the same and set his aside as well. "I want to know what your intentions are when it comes to my son."

"Is this the sort of conversation you had with Lillia?" Fisher asked in return. He wasn't going to give her anything without getting something in return.

"I'm usually the one who asks the questions," the queen said. "I ask, you answer."

Fisher kept his expression neutral. "I'm a police officer. It's my job to ask questions and get the answers I want. I also protect people, especially those I care about."

The queen nodded. "So you care about Franz?"

"Of course I do." He wasn't going to go into any further detail. "But my feelings for him are between the two of us, and I'm not going to discuss them with you before I talk to Reynard about them." They were on completely different pages, even using different names for the same person.

"That's fair enough. But your feelings for my son also affect the crown," she said. "Everything we do has an effect on the monarchy and this institution." She actually smiled. "I know what you did for Franz today. The guards have already given the king and me a report. I know you put yourself between Franz and the reporters when you thought there might be danger. I also know what you told them." She leaned forward. "You're an honest, forthright man who will stand with my son. You have courage and heart. That's obvious. But the question is, will you do what it takes to be part of this family?"

Fisher swallowed hard. "Does this family always rush into relationships like this? I've known Reynard for a few weeks. And yes, being with him is intense. It's like my heart and soul can't get enough of him. But this all seems like an out-of-control freight train."

She nodded. "I understand that. I really do. And no one is asking you to make a decision for the rest of your life at this point. But you have to realize that royal courtships are more public than private. People will want to know, and the press can be relentless. But I think you're more than capable of handling them. Of that I have little doubt." She picked up her cup once more.

"I'm a private person, not a public figure. The reason I fell for your son isn't because he's a prince.

I have feelings for the man under all the pomp and circumstance."

She surprised him. "I know that. Otherwise you and I would be having a very different conversation." She reached to a table and pressed a button. A man Fisher assumed might be a footman entered the room, and the queen turned to him. "Please ask Prince Franz to join us." He nodded and backed out of the room, closing the door once more.

"So is the interrogation over?" Fisher asked.

Reynard's mother smiled and then laughed softly. "For now. Though I will say I'm not used to being cross-examined by anyone." She sipped some more tea. "You have guts, young man, and I like that. You'll need that courage and fortitude, make no mistake about that. But since we're being honest, I think you have what it takes to make a good partner for my son." She leaned forward. "As long as you remember that part of what we do is family and part of it is a job like any other. It can be hard to differentiate between them. But no matter what, being there for my son, backing him up, helping to keep him from falling and from letting the job overwhelm everything—that is part of the deal, and it isn't going away. It never does."

Fisher swallowed hard. "How did you deal with it?"

He watched her eyes as they softened.

"I had to learn. I was born into minor aristocracy, the third daughter of a small, relatively unimportant family with a title and little else. I met the future king, and it was anything but love at first sight. I thought him grand, self-important, and stuffy—because I only saw the official, the duty side of him. It took time for him to show me the man underneath. That's what you already know, so you're further ahead. It's now up to you and Franz, or Reynard, as you call him, to decide what you want." She stood, and Fisher did the same. "Whatever you choose, make it good for both of you."

CHAPTER 17

REYNARD HUNG up the phone with a smile of success and answered the knock on his door.

"Your mother is asking for you." The footman bowed and turned to leave.

He checked the time. Fisher and his mother had been together for nearly an hour, and he had kept himself busy even as he wondered if he was going to have to referee a fight by the time they were done. Fisher could be stubborn, and so could his mother. He stood and went to his mother's sitting room, where he found Fisher and the queen talking quietly together.

"Are you getting along, or is this the quiet between rounds?" he asked as he came in. The footman closed the door behind him.

"Your mother is a very forthright lady. I like that," Fisher said as Reynard took the chair next to him.

"I believe the two of you need to talk. So if you'll excuse me," his mother said and left the room. Holy hell, what exactly had happened during the hour?

"So you survived a talk with the dragon lady," Reynard said. "What did you say to each other?"

Fisher smirked. "I think that's something that should be kept between the two of us. But I believe she gave me her blessing… in a way."

Reynard gasped. "My mother… gave her blessing to the two of us? Jesus, has the world tilted on its axis?"

"No. Your mother wants what every mother or grandmother wants—for their children and grandchildren to be happy. She said that you and I have some decisions to make, and I think this is her way of seeing to it that they get made."

Reynard shook his head. "Are you telling me that my mother is now playing matchmaker? Because that is really out in la-la land." His head began to spin.

"Not really. She gave me some insight into the family, what it is that you all do, and what my role would be should you and I make a go of it." He smiled. "I really like her. She says what she means—at least in private—and we had a frank and sometimes combative conversation. I liked it."

"Okay. Let me get this straight. You went into verbal combat with my mother and lived to tell about it. That has to be a first." Reynard was thrilled. He could see the obstacles between the two of them slowly falling in front of him. But the biggest one still stood, and that was Fisher himself. "So what would you like to talk about?" He'd do just about anything to get Fisher to stay with him.

Fisher drew closer, his gaze heated, movements slow and sensual. "Sometimes words are overrated." He drew closer, and Reynard picked up on the heat radiating off him.

"We can't do this here," Reynard whispered. "There are people just outside the door."

Fisher tugged him into his arms. "Then let's go somewhere we can have our conversation in private." He could almost swear flames danced in Fisher's eyes as he closed the distance between them, taking his lips in a kiss that stole Reynard's breath and threatened to buckle his knees.

THE ENERGY in the room threatened to overwhelm him as soon as the doors to his suite closed behind them. They'd passed a few staff members, but they had all turned away as though they were giving them privacy. Then the walls of Reynard's suite blessedly closed around them, and they were truly alone.

Reynard knew he and Fisher needed to have a real conversation, but at this moment, Fisher was determined to let their bodies do the talking, and Reynard had no intention of stopping him. "I take it—" Reynard began his thought, but Fisher kissed it away as he pressed him down onto the mattress.

"Take off your clothes and lie on the bed, your hands on the headboard," Fisher growled.

Reynard quivered with excitement and complied, shedding his clothes in an instant. "Is this some reaction to all the royal commands?"

"No. It's just because I need you." Fisher removed his own clothes, giving Reynard a show, revealing impressive muscle and a cut belly that he rolled provocatively in a move Magic Mike would envy. Not that Reynard had ever watched the movie. Or at least, he'd never admit it to anyone. Damn, the man was walking sex appeal.

Meeting Reynard's gaze, Fisher climbed onto the bed, straddling his hips before leaning forward to kiss him. "Everyone around here issues orders as though they just expect people to snap to."

"I knew that would get to you," Reynard said, even as he held the antique headboard.

"I'm not a servant, and I'm not going to be ordered around. Neither are you." He smiled and leaned closer. "Unless it's me, and only in the bedroom," he added, his voice barely a whisper, breath tickling Reynard's ear. "In here, we are ourselves."

Reynard nodded, his entire body thrumming with excitement. Here, behind closed doors, he could be himself and just let go. There was no one to impress, and the only one he needed to please was Fisher—and that came as naturally as breathing. He knew him. Hell, when they were alone together, words weren't necessary. Reynard felt what Fisher wanted, and the reverse was also true.

As if to accentuate Reynard's thoughts, Fisher said nothing, using his hands and lips to send Reynard on a slow journey that left every synapse in his brain firing. When they joined, it was intense, mind-blowing, and Reynard held Fisher, their bodies rocking together, Reynard gazing into Fisher's dark eyes, nearly losing himself inside them as their passion built to a peak that neither could maintain. Release came in waves, and Reynard held Fisher tighter, afraid he would fly to pieces until he was anchored.

IT TOOK Reynard a while to come back to himself. When he did, Fisher lay next to him, caressing his shoulder. "I thought I lost you for a while."

Reynard kissed him gently. "I think I lost myself." He nestled closer, slowly closing his eyes. He wasn't sure how long he rested, but when he woke, Fisher looked at him with a gentle smile. "Did you watch me sleep?"

Fisher nodded. "I have to hold these memories while I can."

Reynard sighed. "So you've decided what you want to do."

"What's there to decide? I have a week's vacation, and then I have to go home." He shrugged. "I've had conversations with your family and even your mother, but that's all. I…." He rolled away and slipped out of the bed. "I'm not asking you to ask me or invite me… or whatever it is you have to do. I'm not, because as much as I love you, I don't know if this is something we can do."

Reynard swallowed. "You love me," he said in a whisper, almost like a prayer or a dream that he expected to evaporate like fog on a summer morning.

Fisher leaned over the bed. "Of course I do. How could I not? When we were apart, I thought of you every day. When I saw you again, my heart leapt, and the idea of leaving has me cold. But I'm just the cop who fell in love with a man way outside his grasp. I know that. Sure, things have been fine so far, but like you said, that was just your family. Your mom told me that there is a state dinner next week for delegations from France and Spain. There will be people in glittering gowns and sparkling uniforms. I could never fit in with all that. I can't even afford the clothes to go to something like that." He narrowed his gaze. "Please don't say that if I stayed, you would take care of stuff like that. I could never live that way. I pay my own way and support myself." He swallowed. "This is all just a fantasy, and I guess I'm doing what I did back in Carlisle. Making all the memories I can hold on to before I have to go away."

"You know you don't have to. I want you to stay. I want to find out what's possible between the two of us." Reynard stroked Fisher's cheek. "I feel like part of me is missing when you're gone. What kind of life is that?"

Fisher leaned forward. "It's one we have to figure out how to deal with. When the rose-colored glasses come off, I don't see any other way around it. I don't fit in this world, and I know that." He held Reynard closer. "And before you ask, no one in your family has said anything like that. I think your mom might even like me."

Reynard wasn't going to give up. This was too important to him. "Don't make your decision yet. Please. Keep an open mind. You're here for five more days. Give me that time at least. You said you love me, and I love you too. Don't rush to judgment, because love is worth taking your time." God, that sounded like a line from a bad Hollywood movie, and yet he had actually said it.

"Okay," Fisher agreed, his eyes wide and smile bright. "You're right. We may not have much time, but we both deserve what time we do have."

Reynard breathed a sigh of relief. Now all he could do was hope that the plan he'd put in motion would pay off.

"YOU'RE A NATURAL on a horse," Reynard said. This was their second morning out for a ride, and Fisher really seemed to understand horses and how to treat them. Caesar, in return, acted as though he and Fisher were old friends.

"Thanks. I never thought I'd get to do this." Fisher smiled brightly, his eyes shining. The sun had risen less than an hour ago, and fog hung in low places. The wooded portion of the palace park was stunning in the early morning light. "I really love it."

Reynard kept from pointing out that if he stayed, the two of them could ride together each morning. Instead, he kept quiet as they rode beneath trees that had seen generations of his family pass by either on foot or horseback.

"This looks primeval," Fisher said.

"It is. Most of this land has never been logged or cut. We have people who manage the underbrush, but only in certain sections. Large parts of the land are left natural and have been for centuries. This is some of the last untouched land in the kingdom. We intend to keep it that way. There are many birds and other animals that call this place home." He slowed his horse, and the two of them rode side by side. "I built a treehouse in that one over there. All those branches made for the perfect support. I kept it up for a few years."

"Is it still there?" Fisher shifted to try to see.

Reynard shook his head. "Father had the dean of the park remove all of it so the tree could return to the way it had been. I was surprised my father allowed me to build it in the first place." His dad had been the indulgent one, and Reynard loved him for it. "There's something I want to show you." He veered off and onto a narrow path. "Stay behind me and follow close behind."

"Where are we going?"

"Somewhere pretty special," Reynard called back and then continued forward. They rode through the thickening woods to a clearing before dismounting. "I like to think this space has been like this for a very long time. Nothing grows here but grass."

Fisher took in the open space, maybe forty feet across. "Is that a cave?"

"Yes. We discovered it quite some time ago. I'd love to take you inside, but my father has deemed it off-limits. It's very low, and you have to crawl about twenty feet inside before the area opens up into a room of sorts." He took Fisher's hand and led him to the entrance.

"What are those?"

"Petroglyphs. Markings scored into the rocks. This isn't like the ones in France, but the cave inside has drawings and paintings on the walls dating back fifteen or twenty thousand years."

"How did you find them?"

"I didn't. My grandfather did. He got lost and went inside during a rainstorm. He found the paintings with a flashlight. Scientists came, and they dug out some of the soil that fills the entrance to make the opening bigger and photographed them. Then the cave was closed and the soil allowed to return."

"So now you just leave it?" Fisher asked, squeezing his hand.

"Yes. The past is inside, deep in the earth, and it can stay there." Reynard leaned against Fisher. "I never bring anyone here, and we don't talk about the cave. There are other caves in the area, but this is the only one covered in artwork. It's a little higher elevation, and I think waters may have gotten to the others. This one is dry, so it's preserved. I know I can't show you the drawings themselves, but there are pictures at the palace that I can show you."

Fisher put an arm around his shoulders. "Thank you for bringing me here." Fisher lightly kissed the side of his head. "But other than pictures, I'll never see them anyway. I don't like caves. They scare me."

Reynard paused. "I guess I always thought you were fearless."

Fisher shook his head. "I'm not. No one is. There are a number of things that I'm scared of. Caves are just one thing. I've been inside a few to try to conquer it, but I still don't like them." He met Reynard's gaze. "Right now I'm more afraid of making the wrong decisions and losing things… people. I just don't know how to avoid it."

He blinked and knew exactly what Fisher meant. "We have the same fear." Their gazes locked for a long time, neither of them seeming to find the words to make it better.

"Let's go back," Fisher said as a breeze blew through the trees surrounding the clearing.

"That's the last thing I want to do."

Fisher held him closer, standing still, and Reynard stood with him. Nothing ever stayed the same; Reynard knew that. But there were instances when he wanted to stop time just to make a moment last, and this was one of them.

Reynard lost track of time, but the air had started to warm when they returned to where the horses ate grass at the edge of the clearing. He and Fisher mounted, and Reynard led them back along the path to the main track. Then Fisher spurred his horse forward, and Reynard did the same, taking off through the woods in a race back to the stables along a route the horses knew well. Reynard's horse was faster, but he didn't want to push Fisher, so he stayed behind, letting him win and keeping an eye to make sure he didn't lose control.

"That is so much better than driving fast," Fisher said as he dismounted. One of the grooms led his horse away. Reynard had to agree as he joined Fisher along the path back toward the main palace building. "I've watched people riding fast in movies, but I never dreamed it would feel that way." His cheeks were flushed and his eyes wide and bright.

"Let's go inside. We can have breakfast," Reynard offered, and they climbed the steps at one of the secondary entrances, then changed shoes before heading into the palace proper, where Reynard led the way to the morning room. He opened the door, letting Fisher enter first. He almost ran into him when Fisher paused just inside the doorway.

"Gran, what are you doing here?"

CHAPTER 18

FISHER WASN'T sure what to make of his grand-mother sitting at a table with the king and queen, eating breakfast as though she were at one of her garden club meetings. It was surreal.

"Sweetheart," Gran said with a smile.

Fisher hurried over and greeted her with a kiss on the cheek and a hug. "How did you get here? Why?" His mouth seemed to have short-circuited. He grew quiet, and Reynard managed to get him to sit down to join the others.

"We have a call in a few minutes," the king said with what seemed like a genuine smile. "Cordelia, please make yourself comfortable. It's been a pleasure to meet you. We look forward to dinner and some more of your stories." He and the queen stood, and after each held Gran's hand for a few seconds, they left the room.

"What the hell?" Fisher asked, half under his breath.

Gran just rolled her eyes. "Everyone gets dressed one foot at a time." She took the last bite of her eggs. A footman set down fresh plates, but Fisher was too confused to eat.

"Why are you here?" he asked again.

She set down her fork. "Because I think my grand-son is being a stubborn pain in the ass."

That got his attention. Reynard turned toward the door, and the footmen quietly left them alone.

"I just invited your grandmother to come for a visit." Reynard sounded more nervous than Fisher had ever heard him. "Now, with that, I'm going to leave the two of you to talk." He kissed Gran's cheek, and she fluttered a little before he left the room.

Fisher found himself alone with Gran, and he didn't know what to say.

"I take it you're having some difficulties figuring out what it is that you want." Gran sipped at her coffee with the table manners of a debutante.

"Is that why Reynard called and you got yourself on a plane so fast?"

Gran scowled. "Eat your breakfast. Maybe if you have something in your mouth, you'll talk less and listen more." Fisher purposely didn't comment on how dirty that sounded. "You came over here to figure things out with Reynard. And have you?"

Fisher shrugged.

"Exactly as I thought. You got scared," she said.

Fisher wanted to argue, but he had just taken a bite of toast, and he would have spewed crumbs everywhere. By the time he swallowed, Gran had continued.

"You need to listen to your heart and not worry so much. You were always a responsible boy. I think after you lost your mother you just got quiet and worried that you were going to lose Gramps and me too. But we stayed."

"So I should stay here and… what?"

Gran set down her cup. "Even an old woman with cataracts that the quack of an eye doctor wanted to remove can see that man loves you and that you love him. When he leaves the room, you can't take your eyes off him. And yet you're wondering if you should give a life with him a try." She looked into him as though she had X-ray vision.

"Gran, I know I love him. But—"

Her eyes widened. "Is it worse than I thought—you love the man, but you're just willing to walk away?" She slapped his hand. "I raised you better than that. You don't walk away from love. It may never come your way again." She sipped some more coffee, and Fisher set down his fork. "What do you think? That love is like *Wheel of Fortune* and you get another spin? What if the next time you hit Bankrupt? Or worse, you land on the End of the Line. Game over."

Fisher sighed. "How am I supposed to just leave everything behind and come over here to be the main squeeze of a prince? I don't have a role here, or even a job."

Gran rolled her eyes wide enough to make a teenager proud. "First thing, you can get yourself a job and make yourself useful. You know how to do that. Build a life for yourself—one that includes Reynard and will make you happy. Most of us have to kiss a pond full of frogs to find a prince, and all you had to do was pull yours over at a traffic stop." Now she was just being snarky, but she was also making her point. "You say you don't have a role here. Then find one. What is there back home?"

"You," Fisher said calmly.

"Me? So you're going home just when I've been invited by the royal family of Veronia to work on projects with them?" Her eyes gleamed. "You heard me. Reynard and his brother have said that they have a huge garden and landscape project that they want my help with. Apparently they want the opinion of someone with years of gardening experience." She grinned.

Fisher gaped. It was all he could do. "So you're here to stay?"

"For a while. The neighbors are going to watch the house for me while I'm here, and if I like it, I may sell and move. I'm not too old for an adventure." She sat straighter, her smile radiant. "I feel younger than I have in years."

Fisher could hardly believe it. "You're going to be here for a while and I don't need to worry about you being alone?" This was like a dream come true. "So…."

"All you need to do is follow your heart. I'm fine, and I'm excited to be doing things again. Apparently the position I'm being offered comes with a cottage on the edge of the palace grounds, so I'll have a place to stay and some privacy." She patted his hand again. "So you need to follow your heart."

Fisher got to his feet. "Thanks, Gran," he said as the picture of what he truly wanted came into intense focus. It had always been there in the back of his mind, but he couldn't seem to allow himself to believe it.

"You're welcome. Now go find your prince and sweep him off his feet." She laughed. "I'm an old lady and have been flying all night. I'm going to my room to lie down. Go, go, go."

Fisher hurried out of the room. "Where is Prince Franz?" he asked a footman who was passing. He didn't know, and Reynard hurried down the hall, peeking into open doors before finally finding him in one of the grandest rooms Fisher had ever seen, standing in the middle of a wall of windows, silhouetted against the light. He simply watched him for a few seconds; then Reynard slowly turned around.

"I felt you there."

The impact of those words hit Fisher hard. He took a step forward. "I have to ask. Do you really want me to stay? I need to hear the words."

"More than anything," Reynard said gently. "I hope you aren't mad, but—"

Fisher surged forward, engulfing Reynard in his arms, sweeping him off his feet. "That's all I needed to hear." He kissed him hard, getting just as much energy in return. "I still don't know how this is going to work. I'm just a kid from Carlisle."

"And I'm a prince from Veronia. Together we'll figure it out." Reynard kissed him again, and Fisher's heart flew higher than eagles. This was what he wanted. No more obstacles. He could just let himself go for it, and they'd work things out… together.

Epilogue

"Has it really been a year?" Fisher asked as he and Reynard slowed after nearly flying on horseback over now-familiar paths.

"Yes. A year ago today you pulled me over." Reynard smiled, and Fisher returned it, his spirit light after knowing months of true happiness.

"Did you remember that when you scheduled the garden opening for this afternoon?" Fisher asked, their horses continuing forward at a walk. The first stage of Reynard's public garden project was opening in a gala celebration that the king and queen were throwing in honor of their youngest son's triumph.

"Actually, I hadn't. It was the date set by the committee, and it worked with the royal schedules, so I like to think of it as fate stepping in." There was still a lot to do on the entire garden project, which Fisher believed was expected to take the next decade.

Reynard turned off the path, and Fisher followed.

"Are we headed to the clearing?" He and Reynard had been there only once before, but Fisher remembered this path. Reynard was just far enough ahead that maybe he hadn't heard. Still, Fisher followed, and they dismounted when they reached the clearing. It looked very much the same, with no brush encroaching even though it had been a wet year, fantastic for growing. He had been skeptical about nothing sprouting there, but it seemed it was true. "What are we doing?" Fisher asked as Reynard pulled some things out of his bag.

"You and I are going inside." He tossed Fisher a flashlight.

Fisher looked at Reynard as though he was crazy. "You know I hate places like that."

"Yes." Reynard came close. "But father gave his permission to enter just the once, and don't you want to see it? I checked out the entrance tunnel, and it's about three feet high and a little wider." He took Fisher's hand. "It's up to you."

Fisher closed his eyes, pushing away the rising worry, forcing his courage to the forefront. "Okay. Let's do this." In the past year he had learned royal protocol and survived a number of formal parties and even two state dinners. He'd begun a major project to overhaul and improve palace security. At first the king and queen had been skeptical of the plans Albert and Reynard had asked him to develop, but six months ago, the king himself, in all his finery, had bestowed on him the title of Captain of the Royal Guard. He even got a fancy uniform of his own. There was no way he was going to back down now.

"I'll lead, and you follow behind me. Stay low." Reynard knelt and then moved forward, the light flickering ahead of him. Fisher took a deep breath and followed, sliding into the opening with compressed dirt under him and rock the rest of the way around. At first he wondered what would happen if they got stuck, but he continued forward, moving slowly, breathing through his mouth.

"Take my hand," Reynard said, and Fisher did and was tugged the last of the way, and then he could stand in a twelve-foot rock bubble. The walls were smooth, but as Reynard flashed the light around, he saw only rock—no paint or colors, just gray rock.

Another tunnel led off the back, this one wider, deeper, and thankfully taller. "What do we do if this caves in?"

Reynard took his hand again. "This cave has been here for tens of thousands of years. Come on." He led the way down the next tunnel, which was longer and sloped downward. As they got deeper, the temperature cooled, and Fisher shivered, looking up and to the sides and seeing only rock in every direction.

After a couple hundred feet, the walls broadened and they entered a world of color. The rock itself had changed to various types of sandstone, with pale yellows crossed with reds and even streaks of white. But what made Fisher's heart leap were the paintings, as vibrant and haunting as anything he had ever seen.

"My God," he whispered.

"Yes. While they aren't as vibrant as those in France, or as numerous, these are pristine, preserved by the fact that they were hidden for so long. Only the family, the scientists that examined them, and now you have ever seen them. Father gave us permission to take a few pictures, so go ahead. But understand, they are for us alone."

Fisher nodded. "I know how to keep a secret." There were things that the king himself had shared with Fisher that his sons were not aware of regarding the security measures in and around the palace, and they were the only things he had ever kept from Reynard. He knew this information because of his work, and he kept it to himself the same way he'd expect Reynard to keep privileged information to himself. He was really coming to understand their roles and what was required of both of them.

"I know you do," Reynard said with a smile as Fisher took a few pictures of deer and other animals, some huge. Some he took were close up, while others were farther away. Then he stowed his phone and simply stood next to Reynard.

"This is incredible. It's like we're... I don't know...."

"Getting a glimpse into our own past? These people lived thousands of years ago, and they left behind part of themselves. I bet they had no idea that their artwork would touch people hundreds of centuries later."

Fisher couldn't help feeling like he was being transported across the ages, and yet when he turned to Reynard, he knew he was happy right here in his own age and that he always would be.

Reynard dug into the small canvas bag he'd brought with him. "I know that coming to stay here was hard on you. You left the people and the world you knew behind for me." He seemed nervous. "So I have a surprise for you. Well, two surprises. The first is that I sent invitations to the opening to Wyatt and Quinton, as well as Casey and Bertie and their son. They arrived yesterday and will be at the palace this afternoon. Right now, I have one of the palace liaisons making sure they're settled, and they will be showing them around."

Fisher was stunned. "You did that for me?"

"I wanted you to have friends at the reception, besides Gran, and tonight is going to be a party." Gran had ended up loving Veronia enough that she had sold her home and been offered her cottage on the grounds on a permanent basis months ago.

"You said there was another surprise," Fisher said, unsure what could top that.

Fisher blinked as Reynard went down on one knee. He opened a small box. "Will you, Fisher Bronson, agree to marry me? I want you there with me for the rest of my life. I may have been born a prince, but it is you, Fisher, who is the prince of my heart… and always will be."

In only the glow of two flashlights, Fisher swore he could see the light of a million stars in Reynard's eyes as he said yes.

Keep reading for an excerpt from
Noble Intentions
by Andrew Grey.

CHAPTER 1

"ROBERT," HIS aide, Blake, said as he knocked on the frame beside the open door to Robert's tiny office.

"Am I late for another meeting?" Robert looked up from his computer, where he'd been preparing the documents on a case for a client whose landlord was trying to evict her improperly. The guy was a real piece of work, and Robert was determined to win her some relief from the local council.

Blake chuckled softly. "No."

Robert breathed a sigh of relief and continued typing as fast as he could. He was scheduled to meet with the council in less than an hour, and he wanted to make sure he had all his arguments in place.

"But there is someone here to see you. A solicitor from London." Blake sounded half-breathless with excitement—probably wondering what was going on and if he could increase his stature in the office rumor mill.

Robert closed his eyes and tried to think if he had had any business or clients that would precipitate a visit from a colleague in London. Robert was technically a barrister, trained to argue cases in front of the courts. But here on the edge of Cornwall, Robert had decided that rather than go into high-powered practice in London, he'd become an advocate for those without the means to advocate for themselves. So he'd gone into practice with a few like-minded friends from school, and they'd opened their office on the second floor of a run-down building in Smithford. In their practice, they took everything and did everything. Two of his partners were solicitors, and Robert had learned the ins and outs of that profession as well.

"Give me five minutes, please."

Blake nodded, and Robert put the last touches on the argument and then saved the file. He'd just finished when Blake led in a man about Robert's age, spit-and-polished, wearing a suit that cost as much as Robert made in a month. Robert stood to meet the man.

"Robert Morton? William Montgomery. I'm here on behalf of your uncle, the Earl of Hantford."

"My uncle…." Robert didn't honestly remember having an uncle, but then again, his mother's family had not been the most accommodating when she'd married Robert's father. No one had talked about his mother's family in so long that they didn't register immediately in his memory. "Yes…?"

"Yes. Your uncle, Lord Harrison Hantford, the Earl of Hantford…." He paused. "Apparently the family changed their last name to that of the estate some six generations ago. He recently passed away, and under his will, you are his heir. The estate is entailed, which means your uncle didn't have a great deal of choice in the matter. You are his closest living male heir, and as such you are entitled to the earldom, as well as all the property associated with it."

Robert shivered slightly and blinked in near disbelief. He motioned for Mr. Montgomery to sit down, remembering his manners through the complete shock. "So you're saying I'm the Earl of Hantford now?" He sank into his chair and wondered what kind of holy hell had befallen him.

"Yes, sir. Or I should say, your lordship." Mr. Montgomery seemed to be taking little delight in this.

"Did you know my uncle?" Robert asked.

"I'm afraid I didn't. He was a client with Rhodes, Wentworth, and Middleton for many years, and the task of notifying you fell to me."

"I see." Robert's analytical mind began to kick in. "So what exactly has my uncle left me?"

"There is the family estate, Ashton Park, and a home in London. I'm at a loss to tell you much about them. I haven't seen either property myself, but I will be happy to meet you in the coming weeks to take you to visit them, as well as discuss any arrangements you'd like to make for the properties and contents," Mr. Montgomery said, very businesslike, which was both a relief and unsettling for Robert.

"Can you tell me if the estate is healthy?"

Mr. Montgomery chose that moment to break eye contact, and immediately Robert knew the answer. "I don't know the particulars, but I am under the impression that your uncle lived in the home in London and that he rarely visited Ashton Park. As to more details on the state of the place, we'll have to assess that when we go see it." It was a diplomatic answer, which probably meant that he'd just inherited a huge money-sucking country house with very little means to support it.

"All right." Robert had no idea in hell what else to say. He was a man who made his living with words, and he was at a near complete loss. "Thank you so very much."

"Would you like to meet tomorrow? I can at least take you to Ashton Park so you can see it. I will also have a number of papers and documents that I will need you to sign."

"Is there anyone else who has a potential claim on the estate?" Robert asked.

"No. Your uncle married, but the earl and his wife had no children. I understand from the more senior colleagues in my firm that that was a great sorrow to both of them. However, other than a few impressions and details, I don't have much information to give you. The earl's business was handled by one of our partners who recently passed away unexpectedly, and I'm stepping in to try to fill his rather large shoes." Mr. Montgomery sounded excited about this opportunity, but Robert also saw a touch of fear in his eyes, which would help keep him on his toes. Robert understood that kind of fear; he experienced it on a regular basis. Failure could be lurking everywhere, so it was to be guarded against and held at bay by always being at one's very best.

"All right." Robert pulled up his calendar and figured he could clear part of his schedule for the following day. He arranged a time, and Mr. Montgomery left his office.

Somehow Robert managed to get his mind back on his work, but not without a great deal of effort.

THAT EVENING, after a successful local council meeting that granted him everything he had wanted for his client, Robert pulled up to his mother's small cottage on the outskirts of town. She and his father had saved for years to buy their dream home. His mother, who was approaching seventy, still tended the garden and lovingly cared for the house the way she always had and showed no signs of slowing down.

"How was your day?" She gave him a fright when she popped up from behind one of the garden gateposts, where she had apparently been wrestling with some stubborn weeds.

"God." He stepped back and took a breath to still his heart. "It's getting a little late to be working out here, Mum."

"Pish," she said dismissively. "When you're as old as I am, you take your bursts of energy when you can get them." She dropped the weeds she was holding on the pile she'd collected. "Let's have a cup of tea."

"Good idea." He followed her inside and sat on one of the kitchen chairs, watching his mother put a kettle on. He remembered the dining room furniture from when he was a child. His father had made the table and chairs for his mother as a wedding present, and they had been a part of the family for as long as he could remember.

"What brings you by?" She plugged in the electric kettle and got down the cups and pot so they would be ready.

"It seems that your brother passed away."

She patted the table a few times. "Harrison is dead." She said the words in the same tone that she did when she talked about her neighbor, who she referred to as "the damned old randy bastard" on a regular basis. She smiled for a second and then turned to him. "Christ on the cross."

"You got it in one, Mum."

"But I was disinherited, and…." She sank into the chair across from him. "So my arse of a brother ended up with what he wanted anyway."

"Excuse me?" Robert said, trying to follow all of this.

"My brother was many things—pompous, arrogant, a pain in the arse know-it-all who thought since he had the title, he also had the right to make decisions for everyone else." The kettle was done, and she got up and poured. Robert waited until she was ready to continue. She brought the tea tray with pot and cups to the table and set it down gently. She filled the cups, knowing already how he took it, and handed him his. "My parents died when I was nineteen. So Harrison inherited the title and became head of the family. He thought two things. First, that the title gave him the right to dictate everything about my life. And second, that we'd stepped back a hundred years and that he ruled the damn roost, as well as my personal life. The idiot." She took a sip, pinkie out, as genteel as possible.

"Why didn't I ever hear any of this before?"

She set down her cup. "I dated a friend of my brother's for five years. He was also titled, with a lot of money. Harrison was so excited. He thought we'd marry, but the reason we dated for so long was because I wasn't ready. Then I met your father. George, the guy my brother wanted me to marry, was as pompous as Harrison. He'd hired your father to do some restoration work at his home, and I took one look at him and that was it. Your father stole my heart with a wink, a smile, and one peek at his gorgeous backside." She giggled, and Robert was glad he didn't have a mouthful of tea at that moment.

"So you dumped George and married Dad."

"Yes. In a way. I announced that I wasn't going to marry George and that I loved Peter with all my heart, and Harrison went into a rage. He was always a control freak. Now I think he was deranged and needed professional help. But he hadn't gotten any then. When I didn't back down, he disowned me, and I turned my back on the arsehole forever."

"Mum, I think you're losing me a little."

"I'm getting to the good part. See, Harrison married soon after that, and they supposedly settled down into wedded bliss. But it seemed Harrison had bigger problems. His plumbing wasn't completely functional, and he could never have children." She snickered. "Served the old jackass right, and it's a blessing for the human race. At least his bastardness won't be passed on to anyone else." There was no mistaking her sense of glee at the turn of events.

"Mum!" He had never heard such vehemence from his mother.

"He had the audacity to approach me about returning to the family after your father died—if I let him groom you to take over for him. I told him to stuff it. You had your own life and didn't need the mess that he wanted to heap on you." She sighed. "But he did it anyway. If he weren't dead, I'd wring his neck."

"When was that?"

"About five years ago. He was in one of those regretful phases, but I knew it was a load of garden fertilizer. He never did anything without getting something for himself. And your father had just died, and I thought he was trying to take you from me and…." Her lower lip quivered, and Robert stood to gently place his hands on her shoulders. His mother was many things, but touchy-feely wasn't one of them. She placed a hand on his, and Robert gave her a chance to compose herself.

"Why didn't you tell me any of this before?"

"Because I didn't want you to have anything to do with him. Harrison was an awful man, and we had a good life here. Your father was an amazing provider. He worked hard and made his furniture to help ensure we had some of the extras." She squeezed his hand once, then dropped hers and looked up at him. "I wasn't—"

"It's okay, Mum." Robert waited for her to take a breath. "I wish you had told me, but you're right. We had a good life, and if your brother was as big a jackass as you describe, then we were better off without him."

"But now you're the Earl of Hantford."

"It seems so."

"And everything that goes with it." She turned back to her tea. "I tried to keep you from all that. I really did."

He wasn't sure what his mother was referring to, but it only added to his sense of nervousness. "I'm meeting the solicitor tomorrow, and we're going to the estate. Do you want to come with me?" *It would be really nice not to go alone.* "I'll understand if you'd rather not."

"Where are you meeting him?"

"At my office at one."

"Then I'll go with you. We can meet for lunch, and I'll tell you what I know about what you'll be walking into. Granted, my information is a little out-of-date." She motioned for him to sit, and Robert complied and finished his tea. "This is a burden I had hoped to try to spare you."

"Mum, I'm an earl and I have a peerage…. It's—"

"A burden unlike anything I think you understand." She sighed. "All I wanted for you was a life filled with happiness and the ability to make your own decisions and live your life the way you wanted. Harrison never understood that. He always thought his way of thinking was the only way and that everyone wanted the same things he did. Now he's pulled you into the mess I'm sure he created."

"We don't know the state of things."

"No, we don't. But we're going to find out." She poured another cup of tea, stood, and opened a nearby cupboard. She pulled out a bottle of whiskey and dumped a healthy dollop into her tea.

Things must have been bad. There had been only one other time that he'd seen his mother do that, and it had been the morning of his father's funeral. She had said that she needed some false courage to get through that day, and it seemed she required another dose.

"I'll see you for lunch, though I suspect I'm not going to have much of an appetite."

"I doubt things are as bad as all that." Robert stood and kissed her on the cheek before leaving the cottage. He stopped in the garden on the way out, admiring some of her flowers in the late evening light, and then walked to his car.

ROBERT FELT as though he had been through a meat grinder. He hadn't slept all night and had gone into the office early so he could get as much done as possible. He'd worked with Blake to rearrange his schedule so he could have the afternoon out of the office. Of course, with his mother in the car, he wasn't able to make calls the way he normally would.

The estate was nearly an hour west from Smithford, and he followed William's black hearselike car. His mother had been surprisingly quiet for much of the trip until they turned a corner and the top of a turret broke the skyline.

"That's it."

"When was the last time you were here?"

"Just before I married your father, so over forty years ago." She gasped when Robert made the turn and the estate came into view.

William pulled to the side of the road, and Robert followed. He parked, got out of the car, and walked up to William. His mother decided she wanted to stay where she was.

"That's Ashton Park." William waved his hands in all directions.

"How much land is there with the place?" Robert asked.

"A lot. It's the one true asset of the earldom. There is plenty of land, and from what I can gather from my colleague's notes, your uncle refused to sell any of it, no matter how difficult things got."

"How badly is the place mortgaged?" Robert asked, afraid as hell of the answer. He expected it to be up to the rafters.

"That's the thing. We can't find any record of one anywhere."

"What? You mean I own this pile free and clear?" How in the hell could that be possible? There had to be a catch, and in the back of his mind, Robert latched on to exactly what it could be. "The taxes. Forget I asked."

"Yes, sir. They are going to be steep on the manor house and all the land. However, since your uncle managed to pay the inheritance duties from when he received the estate, you only have the ones to pay for this transfer of ownership."

Like that was a comfort. Instantly upon his uncle's death, Robert owed millions in death taxes on a place he hadn't known existed, other than in some picture he might have seen on one of those documentaries they did on country houses and such.

"Well, we may as well see just how bad a state the old place is in." He tried to think of what he was going to do with it. Selling was the first thing that came to mind—if that were even possible.

"Yes, my lord," William said, and Robert stopped him.

"I'm Robert. Please call me that. I'm not going to stand on all the ceremony and crap, okay? I was Robert before you told me this news and I'm still Robert now."

"Okay." William smiled for the first time. "I'll do whatever I can, Robert."

Robert turned back to the estate and groaned. "Let's go see what we're dealing with." He got back in the car and followed William through the old gate and up the weed-scattered drive, toward the front door. "This place is…." Robert didn't quite know what to say.

"I grew up here," his mother said. "This was my home for much of my younger years."

Robert stopped, and they both got out, the gravel crunching under their feet. The façade of the building looked to be in fine shape. The stone was discolored but appeared intact.

"Is there anyone here?" Robert asked.

"Yes. There is a caretaker on the property. He lives in one of the other homes on the property and sees to it that the building itself remains in reasonable care. But little else seems to have been done in some time." William produced a huge set of keys that looked like something to open a medieval jail. He unlocked the front door and held it open for Robert and his mother.

Robert stepped inside and gasped. All the shutters had been drawn, and everything was covered in sheets and drapes that looked like dusty old ghosts as the breeze from outside fluttered into the hall. Paintings, chandeliers—everything was draped and covered. But even under the dust and sheets, the grandeur of the entry hall shone through.

"My God."

"This used to be…." His mother came inside. "I remember greeting guests as they arrived. Your grandparents were very social people and loved to entertain. It's what this house was built for. Harrison used to love his parties as well, but his took on a very different tone." She walked to the left and pushed open the door to a paneled living room with heavy molding, where a rug lay rolled up to one side. More sheet ghosts and drapes covered everything, and the floor was so dusty, it was hard to see the wood.

Robert looked up and gasped at the frescoed ceiling. "At least that's in one piece. How could anyone just leave all this to rot?" He moved into the living room and through to the next, which was a bookless library.

"What happened to everything? These shelves were full." His mother sounded as though she were going to cry as she wiped her fingers through decades of dust on an empty shelf.

"Apparently they were moved to some sort of storage," William said. "There was a bill for it in the estate records."

Robert lifted his gaze once again and knew the reason for moving stuff to storage. The expansive coffered ceiling was pockmarked with yellow stains. He closed his eyes and groaned. "The roof is going. Some of those stains are recent."

"I did me best, my lord."

Robert turned to find a man in his fifties standing in the doorway, hat bunched in his hands. "Robert Morton." He held out his hand, and the man who Robert assumed was the caretaker stepped forward nervously.

"Gene Parget, my lord. I noticed the room was leaking, so I went up and patched it best I could. I think I stopped the water coming in for now. But some damage was done, mainly in the bedroom above this one. But I don't think I can patch it much more. It needs replacing."

"What about the electrics?" Robert asked.

"That and the plumbing are going too, sir. I don't like to turn on the lights because…." He shrugged. "And the water is off to the entire manor in case of leaks."

"So what you're telling me is that this huge pile of a place needs electrics, plumbing, a roof, as well as…." He raised his eyebrows. "Is there anything that's in good shape?"

"The walls, sir. They're thick and strong, and I repaired the windows last year. Took out the bad ones, reglazed them, and then put them back. I do that every other year."

"What about the kitchen and bathrooms?" When Gene just looked down at the floor, Robert had his answer, and God knew what in the hell he was going to do. "Please show us the rest of the house, and don't leave anything out," he told Gene.

His mother moved back into the living room as Gene led Robert out of the library.

Gene showed him room after room of haunting neglect. Wallpaper peeled from many of the upstairs bedrooms, and the nursery sat frozen in time, like it was waiting for children that had gone and were never coming back. "The summer is humid and the winter cold. I did me best to care for the place, but I'm just me and—"

"It's all right, Gene. You have done the best you could, I'm sure. No one is blaming you for this." He sighed as he looked at the dust and grime covering dinge and neglect.

"Yes, my lord."

"Don't call me that, please." He was never going to get used to that. "I'm Robert. I may have inherited a title, but I believe that men should earn respect, not be given it because they happen to have been born into the right family." Robert turned and wandered through the last rooms, seeing more of the same. The room above the library was the worst so far. The plaster was cracked severely, and parts of the ceiling were in need of stabilization. He didn't go inside and closed the door after a quick peek. "Let's go back down. I think I've seen enough. What other buildings are there on the grounds?"

"There are the stables, which are empty. There's the motorshed, which is also empty. There were greenhouses, but they have fallen down. There are cottages in the village that are part of the estate. They have tenants, and part of their rent agreement requires that they maintain them. I've ensured that has happened. Then there is the park, the thousands of acres around the manor."

Robert nodded, trying to make sense of all this. Mostly what he'd inherited was a money pit. Yes, it wasn't mortgaged, and maybe he could do that, but then he needed the place to generate revenue, which wasn't going to happen with it in this condition.

"Thank you," he said absently. He'd seen more than enough of the mess his uncle had heaped on him.

He met his mother in the hallway, where she peered under sheets and dustcovers. He caught her eye and nodded, and they made their way to the door.

"I know this is a lot to take in and it's going to take some time to get the estate settled," William said as they walked out the front door.

"I know. Not that it's going to make a great deal of difference." Robert needed to figure out what in the hell he was going to do with a place that was so out of step with any sort of modern lifestyle that it threatened to raise a headache the size of London. "Gene, thank you for everything you've done and continue to do. I appreciate it." He shook the caretaker's hand once again and then led his mother to his car. He got in and lowered his window as William approached.

"I'd like to review the rest of the estate details with you soon. There is the house in London, as well as a few other assets."

"Please tell me there is some money somewhere to do something with all this." As overwhelming as all this was, he wasn't above begging if necessary.

"There is enough in various trusts to continue what your uncle was doing. The principal in the trusts can't be touched and it provides an income. I believe that pays for the caretaker and the storage of the books and things. But other than that, no. What money your uncle had, he left to someone else." At that moment, William was as stoic as any good lawyer had to be.

"Okay. I'll need to catch up. Can we meet on Monday?"

William nodded, stepped back from the car, and went to lock the front door of the house.

Robert slowly pulled away. As he drove through the gate, the weight on his chest lifted slightly, but not very much. "What do I do with it?" Robert asked.

"The rooms are still furnished. Almost all of it is still there," she said with a sense of awe.

"All of what?"

"That manor has been in our family for ten generations. You are the eleventh, and the things they collected over the years were all added to the manor. I was afraid Harrison would have sold them, but that probably took more energy than he was willing to spend. So it's all there."

"Okay." Robert turned onto the road back to his office. "So I could sell the furnishings, and break up the land and sell that as well. That would pay the taxes and leave an empty building that could be sold or added to the National Trust if I could get them to take it." He glanced at his mother, who looked about to cry.

"That's your history, my history, and you'd do that without a second thought?" She wiped her eyes, and Robert tried to remember the last time he'd seen his mother cry. He had a hard time doing it. She never cried—stiff upper lip and all that. "You can't just throw it away offhand."

"Then what do I do? I can mortgage the place to the hilt and try to do the repairs that need to be made, but how in the hell do I pay the money back? The estate doesn't have much income, and I can't just open it to tourists and have them flock to the place like it was Downton Abbey. A few people might come, but not enough to make it worthwhile. I could just donate the whole thing to the National Trust and make it their headache, but then everything would be gone." And that was going to break his mother's heart. He could see that.

Robert pulled to a stop at an intersection and waited for a truck loaded with hay to pass before making the turn and continuing on.

"There has to be a way to do something." She was thinking already, he could tell.

"I'm going to have to see what else I've inherited and then try to figure out what can be done." Thankfully the estate wasn't too far away from where he and his mother lived. He could at least continue to live without having to make commutes halfway across the country. "I'm not going to make any decisions today or tomorrow." Robert grew quiet as he drove the rest of the way back to his office.

"I've been thinking," his mother said with a weird smile that Robert was having trouble reading. "You need money to fix up the estate, and you also have a title."

"Okay. I have a title that doesn't help me, other than make me sound like a toff."

His mother leaned closer. "That title comes with a peerage and it has power. People respect the titles. Good or bad, they do, and the title has value."

"Okay. So do I sell it?" Robert asked, knowing he was being ridiculous.

"Of course not. Well, maybe in a way. You do what the aristocracy has always done when they needed money. You marry it."

Robert turned off the engine and blinked in disbelief. "You know I'm gay, Mum. I'm not going to marry a woman."

"No. But I bet there is a gay man with a lot of money who would marry you for the chance to become a count." She held up her hand. "Wives of earls are countesses, so the husband of an earl could be a count.

Think about it. All you have to do is find someone who wants a title and marry him. Of course, he'd have to have piles of money, but you're an earl. Meeting people with money shouldn't be a problem."

He knew his mother was falling in love with the idea. The only problem was that she wasn't the one who was going to have to marry someone for money. Granted, he hadn't had much luck in the love-life department, but still he wasn't particularly interested in selling himself so he could fix up some family estate he hadn't known existed until a few days ago.

"Mum. That's crazy."

"No, it's not. I'm not saying you need to marry some prig you hate. But think about it. Earls and dukes have been doing this sort of thing for centuries. Who knows what you could get out of it? We got bloody Churchill from that kind of relationship. His mother was an American heiress." The more she warmed up to the idea, the more Robert wanted to crawl under the car and hide.

"That's enough. Like I said, I need to see what's in the estate and what my options are before I throw myself off the arranged marriage cliff."

"Who says it's an arranged marriage? There are dating sites and things like that on the Internet. We'll simply find you a gay matchmaker or something, like that show on American television." Her excitement made him more uncomfortable by the second. Where had this idea come from and how did he get it out of her head? "You go ahead and look into the estate. I'm going to go look into some things on my end."

"Mum. Just stop this whole thing right now. I'll come up with a plan to try to figure out what I'm going to do after my trip to the States. I don't need your help getting myself married off to some rich guy for his money. That isn't the kind of life that I want. None of this is."

He could see how his entire way of life was about to change. Up until then it had been the law firm and trying to help people who couldn't help themselves. And now he was supposed to be the Earl of Hantford and all that entailed, including looking after a huge pile of a house because it had been in his family… the family that had disowned his mother. This whole thing rubbed him the wrong way, and all he wanted was a way out of this mess. Selling everything seemed like that way to go. He could be rid of it and that would be that. Pay the taxes, put the rest in trust for the next generation, wherever that would come from, and say to hell with it all.

One look at his mother's set jaw and the gleam in her eyes told him that wasn't going to happen. Not even close. Lord help him—he was going to need it.

ANDREW GREY is the author of more than one hundred works of Contemporary Gay Romantic fiction. After twenty-seven years in corporate America, he has now settled down in Central Pennsylvania with his husband of more than twenty-five years, Dominic, and his laptop. An interesting ménage. Andrew grew up in western Michigan with a father who loved to tell stories and a mother who loved to read them. Since then he has lived throughout the country and traveled throughout the world. He is a recipient of the RWA Centennial Award, has a master's degree from the University of Wisconsin–Milwaukee, and now writes full-time. Andrew's hobbies include collecting antiques, gardening, and leaving his dirty dishes anywhere but in the sink (particularly when writing). He considers himself blessed with an accepting family, fantastic friends, and the world's most supportive and loving partner. Andrew currently lives in beautiful, historic Carlisle, Pennsylvania.

Email: andrewgrey@comcast.net

Website:www.andrewgreybooks.com

Follow me on BookBub

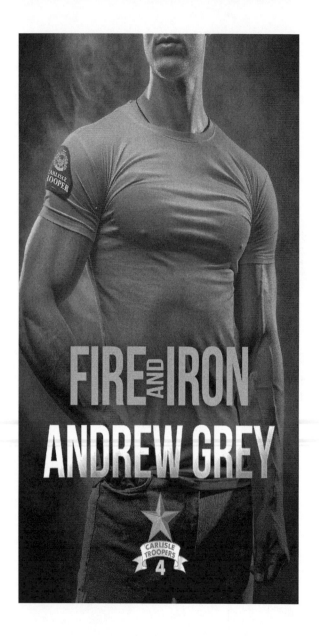

FIRE AND IRON

ANDREW GREY

Preorder the next Carlisle Troopers book now!

A Carlisle Troopers Novel

Gregory Montrose and Fillian O'Connell grew up next door to each other, with a tall fence separating their families.

Fillian, now a state trooper, grew up with plenty of love and little else, looking over the fence at the neighbor's pool he never got to swim in. His family barely made ends meet and he worked hard for everything he has. Including making it to the police academy, graduating at the top of his class, and landing a posting in the Carlisle area.

Gregory had everything growing up, at least on the surface, but it was all for appearances. He looked over the fence at the family who did everything together and listened to his parents fighting most nights. His parents made sure he had all the advantages money could buy, but little else.

A domestic disturbance call reunites them when Fillian talks down a deranged assailant. Both men have changed, and yet they are so very different. Fillian has the life he's always wanted and Gregory is struggling to raise his niece and nephew. Attraction surprises them both, and as heat builds between them, family disasters threaten to either blow them apart or forge them stronger, like steel.

www.dreamspinnerpress.com

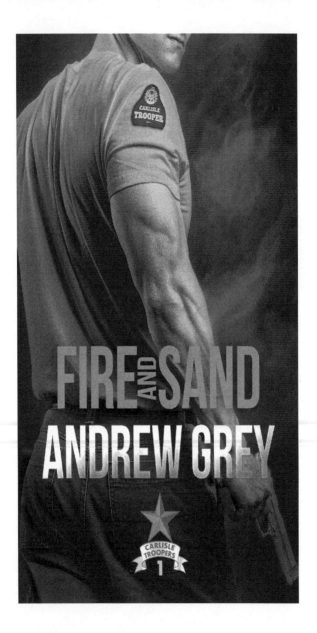

FIRE AND SAND

ANDREW GREY

CARLISLE
TROOPERS
1

A Carlisle Troopers Novel

Can a single dad with a criminal past find love with the cop who pulled him over?

When single dad Quinton Jackson gets stopped for speeding, he thinks he's lost both his freedom and his infant son, who's in the car he's been chasing down the highway. Amazingly, State Trooper Wyatt Nelson not only believes him, he radios for help and reunites Quinton with baby Callum.

Wyatt should ticket Quinton, but something makes him look past Quinton's record. Watching him with his child proves he made the right decision. Quinton is a loving, devoted father—and he's handsome. Wyatt can't help but take a personal interest.

For Quinton, getting temporary custody is a dream come true… or it would be, if working full-time and caring for an infant left time to sleep. As if that weren't enough, Callum's mother will do anything to get him back, including ruining Quinton's life. Fortunately, Quinton has Wyatt for help, support, and as much romance as a single parent can schedule.

But when Wyatt's duties as a cop conflict with Quinton's quest for permanent custody, their situation becomes precarious. Can they trust each other, and the courts, to deliver justice and a happy ever after?

www.dreamspinnerpress.com

A Carlisle Troopers Novel

State Trooper Casey Bombaro works too hard to have time for a love life, never mind a family. But when a missing persons case leads him to three scared kids and eventually their uncle—an old friend from Casey's college days—all that changes.

Bertie Riley hasn't seen his troubled sister, Jen, or his niece and nephews in years. Now suddenly Jen is gone and Bertie is all the kids have. Worried sick about Jen and overwhelmed by his new responsibilities, Bertie doesn't know how he's going to cope. He doesn't expect Casey to step in and lend a hand, but his attraction to his old friend doesn't surprise him. Years may have passed, but those feelings have never gone away.

For the first time in his life, Casey wants something to come home to. Bertie and the kids fit into his life like they are meant to be there. He struggles to balance a budding romance and reassuring the kids with investigating a rash of robberies and tracking down Jen. But when evidence suggests Jen might not only be missing but complicit in a number of crimes, will Bertie and the kids forgive Casey for doing his job?

www.dreamspinnerpress.com

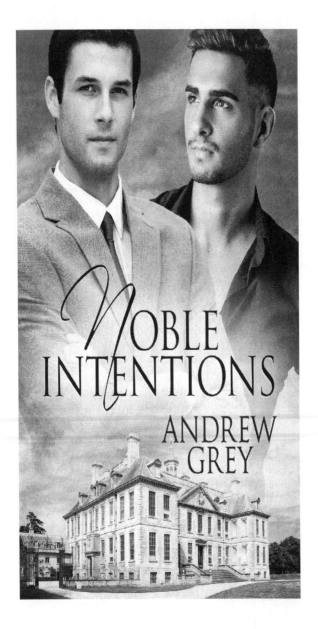

NOBLE INTENTIONS

ANDREW GREY

Robert Morton is in for the surprise of a lifetime. His mother, a bit of a rebel, raised him away from the rest of the family, and it's not until he's contacted by his lawyer about an inheritance that he learns who he truly is: the new Earl of Hantford. His legacy includes ownership of the historic Ashton Park Estate—which needs repairs Robert cannot afford. He'll simply do what the nobility has done for centuries when in need of money. He'll marry it.

Tech wizard Daniel Fabian is wealthy and successful. In fact, he has almost everything—except a title to make him worthy in the eyes of the old-money snobs he went to prep school with. His high school reunion is looming, and he's determined to attend it as a member of the aristocracy.

That's where Robert comes in.

Daniel has the money, Robert has the name, and both of them know they can help each other out. But their marriage of convenience has the potential to become a real love match—unless a threat to Daniel's business ruins everything.

www.dreamspinnerpress.com

TAMING THE
BEAST

ANDREW GREY

"... flat-out wonderful."
—Kate Douglas, author
of the Wolf Tales

A Tale from St. Giles

The suspicious death of Dante Bartholomew's wife changed him, especially in the eyes of the residents of St. Giles. They no longer see a successful business-man… only a monster they believe was involved. Dan-te's horrific reputation eclipses the truth to the point that he sees no choice but to isolate himself and his heart.

The plan backfires when he meets counselor Beau Clarity and the children he works with. Beau and the kids see beyond the beastly reputation to the beauti-ful soul inside Dante, and Dante's cold heart begins to thaw as they slip past his defenses. The warmth and hope Beau brings to Dante's life help him see his entire existence—his trials and sorrows—in a brighter light.

But Dante's secrets could rip happiness from their grasp… especially since someone isn't above hurting those Dante has grown to love in order to bring him down.

www.dreamspinnerpress.com